W9-AYE-706

Praise for *Cross My Heart,*
THE HIDDEN DIARY, book 1

Cross My Heart was *very* descriptive (but not, like, overloaded!) and fun. It's a touching story that a lot of girls can relate to because of their own busy parents. I liked the mystery, too!

> Lilly, eleven years old, daughter of Liz Curtis Higgs,
> author of *Bad Girls of the Bible*

Mama mia! *Cross My Heart* was a great book! I liked the way the author left you hanging at the end of each chapter. It made you want to keep reading. I could really relate to some of the characters, and Claudette made me laugh. You'll love this book! Cross my heart!

> Tavia, ten years old, daughter of Deborah Raney,
> author of *A Vow to Cherish* and *Beneath a Southern Sky*

This book was really good, interesting, and fun. I couldn't say I had one favorite part because I loved the whole book! I couldn't put it down.

> Tyler, eleven years old, daughter of Lisa E. Samson,
> author of *The Church Ladies*

I couldn't put this book down! I guarantee you'll love *Cross My Heart,* and it will keep you on the edge of your seat.

> Marie, thirteen years old, daughter of Terri Blackstock,
> author of the NEWPOINTE 911 series

Cross My Heart is a very exciting book. Lucy . . . meets new friends and learns about God. I know my friends will love this book like I did. Maybe we'll find a hidden diary somewhere, too.

> Madelyn, nine years old, daughter of Cindy McCormick
> Martinusen, author of *Winter Passing*

I think Lucy and Serena are really cool. I can't wait to read the next HIDDEN DIARY book.

> Bethany, nine years old, daughter of Janet Holm McHenry,
> author of *PrayerWalk* & *Girlfriend Gatherings*

Books by
Sandra Byrd
FROM BETHANY HOUSE PUBLISHERS

Take a Bow

SANDRA BYRD

BethanyHouse
MINNEAPOLIS, MINNESOTA

Take a Bow
Copyright © 2001
Sandra Byrd

Cover illustration by Bill Graf
Cover design by Lookout Design Group, Inc.

Unless otherwise identified, Scripture quotations are from the *International Children's Bible, New Century Version,* copyright © 1986, 1988 by Word Publishing, Dallas, Texas 75039. Used by permission.

Scripture quotations identifed NLT are from the *Holy Bible,* New Living Translation, copyright © 1996. Used by permission of Tyndale House Publishers, Inc., Wheaton, Illinois 60189. All rights reserved.

All rights reserved. No part of this publication may be reproduced, stored in a retrieval system, or transmitted in any form or by any means—electronic, mechanical, photocopying, recording, or otherwise—without the prior written permission of the publisher and copyright owners.

Published by Bethany House Publishers
11400 Hampshire Avenue South
Bloomington, Minnesota 55438
www.bethanyhouse.com

Bethany House Publishers is a Division of
Baker Book House Company, Grand Rapids, Michigan.

Printed in the United States of America

Library of Congress Cataloging-in-Publication Data

Byrd, Sandra.
    Take a bow / by Sandra Byrd.
        p.   cm. — (The hidden diary ; bk. 4)
Summary: Friends Lucy and Serena help each other face their fears about being judged by others, and Lucy receives additional guidance from the Bible, as well.
    ISBN 0-7642-2483-2 (pbk.)
    [1. Christian life—Fiction. 2. Friendship—Fiction. 3. Fear—Fiction. 4. Santa Catalina Island (Calif.)—Fiction.] I. Title.
    PZ7.B9898 Tak   2001
    [Fic]—dc21   2001002567

To Peggy King Anderson,

for all she does to enhance and advance

the world of children's literature.

Peggy, take a bow.

Contents

Adventure Times Two

Long before anyone else was up, Lucy peeked out her bedroom window. Morning cracked open, spilling yellow and white light across the pale sky.

It was Saturday, the beginning of another diary adventure.

Lucy's fingertips tingled at the thought.

Kitty-corner across her backyard was Serena's house. Long black phone wires hung like licorice ropes between the houses. Lucy could almost imagine them crackling as she thought about the phone conversation they'd soon have. They'd plan when and where to meet, and Serena would bring the old diary and the yellow umbrella. According to the diary entry they'd read the previous afternoon, this week's adventure would be daring.

Now Lucy's toes tingled, too.

She ran into the bathroom to take a quick shower. She wanted to be ready when Serena called. The water ran cold for a long time; even the hot-water heater wasn't awake yet. After brushing her teeth and running her hand through her red-gold curls, Lucy ran back into her room and tossed on a pair of jean shorts and a T-shirt. She put on her rings and necklace, then slipped on her flower-power sandals. Someone—her mom or dad—was rustling a newspaper downstairs.

Sooner than she'd dared to hope, the phone rang.

"Hello?" Lucy plopped on her bed with the portable phone.

"Lucy, it's me, Serena."

"Hi! I've been waiting."

"I hope it's not too early, but . . ." Serena paused. "I've had a little change of plans."

"What?"

"My family is going to Knott's Berry Farm today—you know, the amusement park?"

"Oh." Lucy had forgotten.

"All four of us were going to go. Now Roberto is staying home because . . . well, because of something. My dad's going to stay with him."

"What's wrong with Roberto?"

"I'll tell you later," Serena rushed on. "What I wanted to say was, my mom said you could come with us if you want. She'll meet my aunt there, so she'll have someone to talk with. And if you come, I'll have someone to go on the rides with."

Lucy leaped from her bed. "Let me go and ask my mom!"

She raced downstairs, taking the phone with her. Her mom sat at the kitchen table drinking coffee, her bathrobe touching the tops of her pink slippers.

"Mom, Serena wants to know if I can go over town with them today to Knott's Berry Farm!"

After talking with Serena's mother, Lucy's mom hung up the phone. "You'll have to hurry." She pointed at the clock on the microwave. "They want to take the next ferry."

"I'm practically ready." Lucy stashed the money her mom handed her in her wallet. Then she ran into the small piano room. On top of the piano sat a small tape recorder. Lucy pressed Record, then she sat down and began to play the Beach Boys' song "California Girls."

"What are you doing?" Lucy's dad hurried into the room. "I thought you were going to Knott's Berry Farm!"

"Dad!" Lucy turned the tape recorder off and rewound it. "Now I have to start over. I *am* going to Knott's Berry Farm. But I wanted to take a little present to Serena to thank her for inviting me today. She loves this song."

Dad squeezed Lucy's shoulder. "Well, get going. You'll need to leave in ten minutes." He rumbled back toward the kitchen and Lucy's mother.

Lucy pounded out the tune again, stood up, and clicked off the tape recorder.

Perfect. Well, it should be. I've played it about a thousand times.

Lucy's mother handed a sweat jacket to Lucy and kissed

her good-bye. "We'll meet you at the ferry tonight. Have a good time. And take these." She handed the two walkie-talkies to Lucy. "Serena's mother can take one and you girls can take the other. Then I'll know you're okay."

Lucy smooched her mom's cheek, grinning at the slightly sticky spot of Melon Madness lip gloss she'd left there. Then she ran out the door.

She headed up the block, around the corner, then down the street just a few houses to Serena's. The plaque on Serena's door said *Saludad, Amigos.*

Welcome, friends.

Lucy smiled. Her summer friend.

Serena opened the door as soon as Lucy knocked.

"I've got the diary," she whispered. "We can read it on the way over, and then my mom will keep it with her stuff for the rest of the day."

Ah yes. Two fabulous adventures.

Lucy handed the cassette she'd made to Serena.

"What's this?" Serena turned it over.

"Remember last week when you walked in on me playing the piano? And I stopped?"

Serena nodded.

"I was too embarrassed to keep playing in front of you then, so I recorded it. We *are* California girls, at least for the summer." Lucy giggled and Serena joined her. "I wanted to do something nice for you, too," Lucy finished.

"Thanks! It'll be safe here till we come back." Serena set it on a hallway table.

"Let's go, young ladies!" Mr. Romero stepped into the

hall. Serena's dad worked on the mainland, so Lucy only saw him on weekends.

After shuttling the girls and Mrs. Romero to the dock in the family's golf cart, Mr. Romero returned home. Catalina Island, where they all spent the summer, was a scrap of an island twenty-six miles off the coast of Los Angeles, California. It would take about an hour on the ferry to get to the mainland, and then a quick drive with Serena's aunt to Knott's Berry Farm.

Lucy looked around the boarding area, hoping that no one else they knew would be on the ferry—especially Julie, who had seemed to hate Lucy since the day she'd arrived.

But Julie wasn't there, nor anyone else they knew.

Yahoo!

Lucy and Serena walked up the ramp, found some empty seats, and settled in as the ferry pulled away from the dock and into the blue channel waters.

"So why couldn't Roberto come?" Lucy whispered.

Serena looked toward her mother, a few chairs away, reading a magazine. "Well, he's entered the Island Art Fair this week. His band is performing." Serena pointed to a poster on the wall of the ferry advertising the fair, which was to be held on Friday.

"Yes?"

"Anyway, he's really stressed out. His grandma is coming to watch them play for the first time ever. He hasn't seen her in a few years."

"You mean, *your* grandma?" Lucy wrinkled her forehead.

Serena looked into Lucy's eyes. "Roberto is my half

brother. I think I told you that once."

"I'd forgotten," Lucy said. "He had a different mother, right?"

Serena nodded. "His mother died when he was a baby, and a couple of years later my dad married my mom. My mom is his mom, too, now. But he still has those other relatives. He really wants to impress his grandma. So he's staying home to practice with his band."

Lucy looked at the Island Art Fair poster.

Join us for a display
of the best young artwork and music
this side of Paris!
All performances and exhibits
by the talented 12- to 18-year-olds of Avalon.

"I hope he does okay," Lucy said. "Playing music in front of all those people would give me a heart attack."

"Me too."

"I see they have artists there, too," Lucy pointed out. "Twelve-year-old artists."

Serena frowned. "Yeah, right. Let's read the diary, okay?"

"Okay!" Lucy said. "I'm totally excited to plan our adventure this week!"

Serena dug the diary out of her bag. "Do you think my great-grandmother ever imagined that seventy years after she and her best friend wrote this diary, you and I would be copying them?"

"Nope," Lucy replied. "But I bet they'd think it was cool." Each week she and Serena read a section in the old diary. Somehow, some way, they did something similar to what the original diary writers had done. No matter what.

"Oh no. We don't have our umbrella," Serena said.

Hmm. They always read the diary under Serena's bright yellow umbrella.

Lucy looked around the boat. As she spied the snack bar, a slow smile spread across her face.

"Wait here," she said, then made her way toward the front of the boat. She held on to the seats on either side as the choppy water rock-and-rolled the ferry.

"A Coke and a Dr Pepper, please," Lucy ordered. As the attendant filled the glasses, Lucy pointed at some mini paper umbrellas with bright cherries skewered on their spiky stems. "And may we each have one of those? Yellow?"

The lady nodded and put a yellow paper umbrella into each cup, next to the straw. It was tricky getting back to their seats without spilling anything, but Lucy did it.

"Voilà!" She took her umbrella out of her drink and leaned her head near Serena's. Then she popped the tiny umbrella over both of their heads. "A yellow umbrella."

Serena laughed and drew the diary out of her bag. She opened it to the page just following the one they'd last read and took out two yellowed airline tickets.

Serena always read the parts that her great-grandmother—also named Serena—had written, and Lucy always read the parts that Mary had written in her curlicue writing.

Serena started.

"Dearest Diary,

We told you that this week was going to be a bit of a dare. Mary and I have been reading everything we can about Amelia Earhart. She is our hero. So bold! So brave. But then Mary had a dotty idea."

Lucy took over the diary at that point, reading Mary's words.

"It is not dotty! They're offering airplane rides from Avalon to the mainland and back, and my father promised us a ride if we'd like one. Why not be like Amelia Earhart? Let us see what it's like. I have to admit, when I see those squawky steel birds looping and drooping, my stomach does the same. No one we know has been on an air ride yet. No one."

Lucy grinned as she handed the diary back to Serena, who finished the installment.

"My brother has insisted that we ride, because he can't go if I don't go. It's so daring that it really gripes my mother's soul. We'll be back to tell you how it goes. I really do want to go, and Mary is helping me overcome my fear. I'm afraid, and Mary is, too, though she won't admit it. I hope we don't get airsick. Or scream in front of the other passengers. Or cry or refuse to get back on for the return flight. How would we get home then? more later.

> Faithful Friends,
> mary and Serena."

Serena closed the diary as Lucy unpopped their mini-umbrella.

"An airplane ride to the mainland isn't daring anymore. I guess we'll *have* to do something daring," Lucy said. "Something we're afraid to try, but must. Like them!"

As soon as Lucy mentioned the word *daring*, she noticed Serena's face grow pale. All of a sudden Serena changed the subject.

"Let's think about it later. We have till Friday." Serena quickly unfolded a Knott's Berry Farm brochure. "Let's plan the rides we want to go on." She pointed out the route as Lucy looked over her shoulder.

"Let's definitely go on the Mexican Hat Dance."

"And GhostRider," Lucy said.

"And the Calico Mine Ride," Serena finished. "I . . . I don't know about Montezooma's Revenge. But the only one I'm truly afraid to go on is Supreme Scream. So we're going to skip that one."

Lucy's eyes were drawn to Supreme Scream on the map. A shiver ran up her back. She'd always wanted to ride it.

Supreme Scream

Saturday afternoon . . .

When they got off the ferry a few minutes later, Serena's aunt Margie was waiting for them. She wore a funky skirt and strappy sandals and had sunglasses like a movie star's. Lucy's aunts wore sensible shoes and drove dented mini-vans.

"Hey, girl!" Aunt Margie ran up and threw her arms around Serena.

As soon as she spied Lucy, Margie ran over to hug her, too. Then she took Mrs. Romero's hand, and the four of them got into Margie's car.

"Ready for a day of fun?" she asked as they motored toward the park.

"Yes!" Serena said. "Lucy and I will plan it all out."

Serena's mother laughed. "Margie and I are going to sit and eat and chat and shop. I don't get to visit with my little sis very often."

"But maybe we'll meet you girls for one ride later," Margie said with a grin.

They got to the park and paid, giving Mrs. Romero one walkie-talkie and sticking the old diary in her purse for safekeeping. They planned to meet later for a big dinner together.

Serena grabbed Lucy's hand and led her down the smooth walkway to the right.

"Can we go to Camp Snoopy first?"

Lucy was kind of hoping for GhostRider. The lines were so long, she worried about getting all the rides in. But Serena was the hostess, after all. Lucy smiled. "Of course."

They went on the carousel first and then the Ferris wheel. When they reached the top, Serena scanned the other rides in the park. "I really wish I weren't so afraid. I wish I could go on the scary ones more often and not always stick with the baby rides."

Lucy decided right then and there to help her friend's wish come true, just like Mary had done for Serena in the diary.

"How about if we try something medium scary?" she asked. "I'll be right with you, and it won't be bad. Okay?"

Serena frowned. "Well, okay. I'll try."

They lined up at GhostRider, a roller coaster.

"Let's get out of line. It's too long." Serena looked worriedly up at the coaster.

"Roller coaster rides are short, so the line will go quickly even if it's long," Lucy said. She smiled warmly at Serena as they stood at the tail of the snaking line. Serena still looked as if she might dart out of line.

Lucy placed her hands on the wooden rails on either side that guided the would-be riders. As they got closer to the GhostRider entrance, screams rolled up and down the coaster tracks. Finally the girls moved forward and slid into the seat of the wooden bucket they would ride in.

They clicked their seat belts in place, grasped each other's hand, and gripped the cold silver safety bar with their free hands. The bucket yanked up the metal tracks. And before they could add their screams to the wild choir, their bucket dropped straight down.

Afterward, when they had gotten off, Serena said, "Well, it wasn't *too* bad." They giggled together.

After GhostRider Serena chose the Mexican Hat Dance twirl ride. After getting thoroughly dizzy, they waited forever for Bigfoot Rapids. Then the girls strolled past a Snoopy boutique.

"Let's buy something together," Lucy suggested.

"Okay." Serena checked in with her mother through the two-way radio, and then they walked into the store. After looking over Snoopy earrings and Peppermint Patty candies, the girls settled on two stuffed Woodstock birds.

"I like him." Serena snuggled her little Woodstock.

"He's nice, like you," Lucy agreed, patting his yellow fur. "And cheerful, like me!"

They found some key chains to buy so they could attach their Woodstocks to their shorts pockets and would not have to carry them all day.

After that they found a food place and kept company with two greasy burgers, a large Dr Pepper, a large Coke, and a tangle of French fries.

Her stomach full, Lucy wanted to help Serena build up courage. "Let's go on Montezooma's Revenge next."

Serena took a deep breath. "I don't know. It looks very scary to me."

"It will be okay, really. And when the day is over, we'll have had tons of fun and you'll have your wish not to be afraid anymore. Do you want to go on?"

Serena held Lucy's gaze for a long minute before nodding. "All right."

The girls walked through the funnel-cake stands, around the Butterfield Stagecoach station, and past the carousel to park themselves at the end of the Montezooma's Revenge line.

"I never wanted to go on this. But I will this once, since you're here with me," Serena said.

Lucy hugged her friend. "It will be fun, you'll see."

The girls finally had their turn on the ride. It went forward at what seemed like the speed of light, and then backward with their full tummies lagging behind them. A loop in the middle topped off the adventure.

Both of them wobbled off the ride.

"It was kind of fun," Serena admitted.

"You were so brave!"

Lucy opened her park map and saw the ultimate ride: Supreme Scream.

"I have it," she said.

"Have what?" Serena asked.

"Your daring Diary Deed. You can come with me on Supreme Scream!"

Serena sat down on a nearby bench. "Ahhhh, no."

Lucy sat near her. "It'll be okay. It's not too bad. We'll be together, and it will be awesome."

"Not too bad?! How do you know? Have you ever gone on it?"

"No," Lucy admitted. "But I would never want anything to hurt you."

"It's a straight drop down. Like ten stories or something. I'm not going. It won't even be fun, so why should I?"

"Well, it's daring," Lucy said. "Look, it's a Diary Deed. You'll be so proud of yourself after you do it. I promise."

Serena stood up and began to shuffle forward so slowly, Lucy wasn't sure if she was really moving at all. "I guess. Let's go."

They got at the end of the long line, and Lucy chatted about anything she could think of to help Serena not be scared. Serena's face looked as if all the blood had gone south. She kept pulling on her ponytail over and over, making it tighter.

I'm doing the right thing, Lucy reassured herself. *It's good to help her overcome being afraid. She wanted to overcome it—she said so! She'll be so happy afterward and even more brave in the future, brave enough to do whatever she wants.*

They got closer and closer to the front of the line. Lucy couldn't take her eyes off the riders. Supreme Scream was a tall tower of a ride. Riders were strapped into individual seats, secured across the chest and the legs. Slowly, the chairs rose to the top of the tower—you could hardly make out the waving arms of those brave enough to hold them above their heads. All those waving arms looked like an upside-down octopus in trouble.

"Hear those screams?" Serena whispered.

Lucy nodded. Two boys ahead of them ditched the line.

Suddenly the seats dropped at full gravity force, all the way to the bottom of the tower. Then it bounced back up and fell again, then again. Finally the eight victims were let free.

Lucy hoped she'd get a yellow seat and that hers would be next to Serena's and not around the tower's corner.

"I'm not going to do it." Serena hesitated for a moment, then stepped out of the line. As she did, she looked over her shoulder. Lucy saw hope in her eyes. She knew that Serena wished she'd leave the line, too. Lucy turned her back. She wished Serena had stayed with *her.*

If I stay, maybe she'll come back in line with me.

But Serena didn't come.

Maybe she's afraid they'll think she's cutting in line.

Still Serena didn't come back.

Lucy headed toward the yellow seat she'd hoped for, but she didn't really care about it anymore.

After being strapped in, Lucy scanned the crowd for Serena. The drop was amazing, but Lucy didn't smile or let loose a crazy yell. After the third bounce, she waited till the ride came to a complete stop and hopped out.

Serena is probably waiting by the ride entrance. Lucy headed over there. Streams of people lined up, some stood to the side, waiting for friends or family. She saw lots of blond heads, some redheads, and one boy with green hair. A few black-haired girls. But none of them were Serena.

Maybe she's sitting on a nearby bench! Lucy circled the

ride, scanning all around her, anywhere that a person might wait for someone. Crowds of excited friends clumped together. Lucy saw a young family keeping track of zany toddlers with kiddy leashes. An old lady fanned herself under a palm tree.

No Serena.

Maybe she'd gone to the bathroom!

But she didn't come back.

Lucy slumped onto one of the benches and squeezed her little Woodstock as she realized what had happened.

Serena had deserted her.

Mementos

Late Saturday afternoon and evening . . .

Lucy parked on the hard bench for another five minutes, hoping to see Serena walk by. Finally she got up and walked around again.

If Serena didn't come back soon, Lucy would have to do something. But what? Page Mrs. Romero over the park intercom? Explain to her that they got into a fight over a ride? *Uh-uh.* If Serena didn't show up in ten minutes, Lucy guessed she'd call her mother. Mom would know what to do.

Lucy sat down at the entrance to Supreme Scream again.

As she stared ahead of her, she felt a hand on her shoulder. She turned around.

Serena.

"Hi." Lucy said.

Serena sat down next to her. "Hi," she answered. Neither spoke for another minute. There were at least six inches separating them on the bench.

"I thought you'd left for good," Lucy said, more mad than worried now that Serena was back.

"My mom paged me on the walkie-talkies to see if we needed more money," Serena said. "I thought I'd go and get it while you were riding Supreme Scream."

"Oh."

"Also," Serena continued, "I wanted to get back at you for trying to make me go on the ride and then for staying on when I got off. I'm really sorry," she finished. "The ride is just not me."

Lucy looked at her friend, her heart melting fast. "No, *I'm* sorry for pushing you. I thought it would make you feel good to overcome your fear. I went too far."

Serena said nothing, so Lucy continued. "I guess we had our first fight."

"I guess we made up from our first fight, too," Serena said.

Lucy smiled and scooted closer to Serena on the bench. Serena leaned over and hugged her for a second.

Things didn't feel exactly the same as they did before the fight, but they were on the road back, anyway.

"I did get some money," Serena said. "Want to go and spend it?"

Lucy stood up and giggled. "But of course!" They each bought a frozen lemonade and headed toward the old-fashioned Ghost Town area.

"Let's get our pictures taken in the old-time photo booth," Lucy said. Serena nodded and grabbed Lucy's hand.

When they walked in, Lucy asked, "Do you have any clothes like girls would have worn in 1932?"

"Great idea!" Serena said.

The man helped them find long, narrow dresses and big, wide hats. "A lot of girls had bobbed hair then," he said. "It was very fashionable."

"I am *not* cutting my hair!" Lucy said, and Serena nodded in agreement.

They headed into dressing rooms to change, and when they came out, Serena said, "You look like Mary must have looked."

Lucy was wearing a white gown with a flare at the bottom, and when she pulled it to her knees she showed off the button-up boots beneath. "That's because I read her parts in the old diary, right?" Lucy giggled. She nearly tripped over the long dress. "Whoa!"

Serena stared at herself in the mirror. "Do you think my great-grandmother looked like this?" Serena wore a red dress with a wide sash and a hat that pulled down over one eye.

"I don't know," Lucy said. "But let's get an extra picture for your Grandma Peggy and ask her. She was so nice to let us have the diary, after all."

The photographer took several shots of them. After changing back into their own clothes, the girls waited in front of the booth while the pictures were developed. They bought one for each of them, one for their own best-friend's diary, and one for Serena's grandma. After panning for gold and listening to an Old West story, they went to meet Serena's mom and aunt for dinner.

The line that wrapped around Mrs. Knott's Chicken Dinner Restaurant was longer than the lines at many of the rides. The air was heavy with the aroma of fried chicken and gravy. Serena aimed her nose to the air. Lucy's tummy grumbled.

"I guess it's worth the wait," she said. Finally they were seated at a table in the restaurant. "Look, it says it seats two thousand people!" Lucy said. She looked around the country-kitchen-style room.

"We would have fit in here with our 1932 clothes," Serena said.

After they ordered, Mrs. Romero asked, "How was the day, girls?"

Serena told her about Montezooma's Revenge, the old-fashioned pictures, and the little Woodstocks and key chains. Lucy talked about GhostRider.

"Any trouble?" Aunt Margie asked.

Lucy looked at Serena. Then Serena shook her head.

"Nothing major," she said. Thankfully, the adults didn't press the subject.

While they waited for dinner to arrive, Serena pulled some crayons out of a plastic cup in the center of the table and doodled on the paper tablecloth. Lucy was about to ask Serena if she wanted to play Hangman. Instead, she watched Serena sketching. The sketch was simple—a vase with flowers. Some flowers stood straight up, their faces seeking the sun. Some tilted to the side, tired. A few flowers hung their heads, ashamed. The colors worked together in a way they never did when Lucy used crayons.

Suddenly Lucy had a brilliant, scary idea. She knew

what Serena's Diary Deed should be. *Must* be. And it would be doing something good for Serena, too. Their friendship had nearly recovered from the first fight. The question was . . . was their friendship strong enough to stand another suggestion?

Lucy tiptoed into the conversation.

"You draw so well," she said. "And I see good art all the time, since my mom is an artist."

Serena looked up, self-conscious and seemingly embarrassed by her little flower family and their glass-vase home.

She pulled her napkin over the picture. "Let's talk about something else," she said.

The waitress brought their meals, and the girls dug in.

Lucy would have to bring the subject up again. But when? They'd promised to do something like the diary girls did each week, no matter what.

After dinner Margie spoke up. "We have time for one more ride before I have to get you back to the ferry. How about the Supreme Scream?"

Both girls stopped walking.

"You're not afraid, are you?" Margie said. "It looks like such fun."

Lucy looked at Serena, who seemed unable to speak.

"I'd rather go on something calm like the log ride," Lucy spoke up. "If it's all the same to you."

"Sure!" Margie said. "You're the guest. I can go anytime."

As they headed over to the ride, Serena reached out and squeezed Lucy's hand.

"I'm going to try to always do good things for you,"

Lucy said. The unspoken new Diary Deed she'd planned popped uninvited into her mind.

"Me too, for you," Serena said.

Not another word was spoken. Yet . . .

🍂 🍂 🍂

After the ride they left the park, and Margie drove them back to the ferry. By now it was nearly dark, and they climbed onto the boat in their slightly damp shorts—a result of the log ride.

Mrs. Romero took a seat by the window; the girls sat across the aisle from her. Few other passengers rode the late ferry.

The boat backed out of its berth and into the open channel. The water was choppier tonight, and the girls bounced a bit in their seats. Lucy wasn't afraid of water. But she couldn't help wondering if these light boats ever tipped over.

She glanced up at the Island Art Fair poster, and her stomach clenched. More likely there was rough water ahead in other ways. She might as well dive into the conversation.

"Did you see that the last day to sign up to exhibit is Monday?" Lucy nodded toward the poster.

"Yeah," Serena said. She handed the two-way radios back to Lucy. Lucy clipped them onto her shorts next to Woodstock.

"Well, I remember a couple of weeks ago you said your mom and your brother wanted you to enter. Like your brother is."

"Yeah, but I didn't," Serena said, her face still calm. She obviously didn't guess where Lucy was steering this conversation.

"I think you should enter. Your art is really good," Lucy said. Serena looked up in alarm.

By now the boat was cresting big waves, rolling up and down. The few people who had been sitting on the outside deck came in, and the captain asked that they all remain seated.

"Entering the Art Fair would make a good, daring Diary Deed," Lucy finished. She held her breath.

Serena's face clouded over. "I thought you said you were only going to do what was good for *me*! Unless you think being told by professionals my art stinks is good for me. I did that once at school. I told you about it, remember?"

Lucy nodded. "But—"

"Let's not talk about it. I feel seasick," Serena said. She put her head down.

Lucy closed her eyes tight.

A short while later they arrived at the dock. Serena's mother stood next to them as they waited to get off, so they had no private place to talk. Lucy's parents met them at the end of the ramp.

"Ready to go home, Sparky?" her dad asked.

"Yes," she said. She thanked Mrs. Romero and said good-bye to Serena. She couldn't read her friend's feelings.

If Serena had her mood ring on, it would probably be red.

Later that night in her bedroom, Lucy unpacked everything from her day. She set Woodstock on her bed next to

Tender Teddy. She propped one old-time picture on her dresser and slipped the other one into the best-friend's diary she and Serena had been writing in. They wanted to spend the summer writing adventures in their *own* diary, just like the 1932 girls had done in theirs.

Lucy looked down at their book and stared at all the blank pages yet to be filled in.

Doubt Wiggles In

Sunday morning . . . D Day minus five

Sunday morning arrived, and Lucy's first thought was of Serena. She peeked out her window, hoping Serena's curtains would be pulled back. They weren't. Lucy let her own curtains fall closed. Maybe Serena was still asleep.

Lucy's second thought was that this was a church day, and she had only two dresses. She'd already worn one of them last week, her first week at church in years.

She opened her closet and pulled out the light blue crepe dress her parents had given her for her twelfth birthday a couple of weeks ago. When she put it on she felt older. Fourteen, at least. After shaking the bottom of the dress so that it fell smoothly, she stood in front of her dresser, looking in the mirror. She glimpsed the reflection of her new plant, which was already wilting—not even a week since she got it. All her life her houseplants had died—and she was trying to figure out why. This week she was experimenting by replacing the water with something else. But maybe it didn't like Dr Pepper as much as she did. She'd try coffee, maybe, next time it was dry. Or orange juice. Orange juice was really healthy.

Lucy smoothed some lip gloss on, rearranged her hair, and headed downstairs. Her low heels *click-clack*ed on the wooden steps, announcing her arrival.

"You look lovely," her mom said as Lucy entered the kitchen.

"Thanks," Lucy said. "Anyone call this morning?"

Her mom shook her head. "No."

"Oh."

"We'll be leaving in a few minutes," Lucy's dad said, grabbing his Bible from the table. "Do you want to get your Bible?"

Lucy hadn't yet opened the Bible her parents had given her at the beginning of the summer. "You always bring yours. I'll just share."

Her parents exchanged glances. "All right," Mom said. "Would you like to invite Serena over for lunch after church?"

Lucy peeled a piece of nail polish off of her thumbnail and stared at it intently. "I think I'll wait till she calls me first."

"Is there a problem?" her dad asked.

Lucy stood up. "I just want to wait for her to call me first. I'll be on the porch."

"No breakfast?"

"No thanks."

The salty morning breeze misted Lucy's hair. The swing rocked back and forth, the motion comforting, like a mother rocking a baby in her arms. Soon Lucy's parents locked the door behind them, and they all walked the few blocks to their cozy little white-and-green church with its lawn full of cheery yellow flowers.

Right off, Lucy knew this week would be different. Jake stood at the church entrance!

Jake was a new . . . ah, friend. His family owned the ice-cream and candy shop in town, and he seemed as sweet as the stuff in the store.

"Good morning." He handed Lucy a bulletin from the small stack in his hands. She took it from him, being careful not to touch his hand in the process.

"Good morning, young man," Lucy's dad said. "I remember you. We met when the puppies were born last week. Jacob, right?"

Jake nodded his head, and Jake's dad, who was on the other side of the church's entry, introduced himself, as well.

Finally they sat down, Lucy between her mom and dad.

"Mom!" Lucy whispered. "Look who's singing!"

Rachel, the teenaged girl who had first welcomed Lucy to the church, stood in front. She used no microphone. The church was small and her voice was strong.

As Rachel ended her song, Lucy sighed, feeling closer to God than ever.

Her mother leaned over. "That's one song you and I can both agree on," she said. Lucy giggled. She and her mom almost never liked the same music.

"Open your Bibles, please," the pastor began. In Lucy's row everyone fluttered to the passage marked in the bulletin. Everyone except Lucy, that is. Even young Claudette had her own Bible. Lucy looked forward and over one row to where Jake sat. His Bible was black.

Lucy's dad held his Bible over his lap so she could look on.

Some of the time Lucy listened. Some of the time her mind wandered. But when the pastor called Rachel his daughter, Lucy's ears tuned in like an FM radio.

"Just like my daughter, Rachel," he'd said.

"So *that's* why she's here today," Lucy whispered to her mom. "'Cause I know she works at the Christian camp on the Island!"

"Shush!" her mother whispered.

Lucy sank low in the pew. She kept listening hard, though she missed some of what the pastor had said.

"The Bible is like a letter. God's letter to you, written long ago but just as meaningful today as it was when it was written. Written by God through real people back then who had questions and fears and joy and hope. Written for real people today with questions and fears and joy and hope. He wants to talk with you every day. Through prayer. Through people. Through song. Through His Word."

Lucy peeled back the polish from another nail. Was it possible to have fear and joy at the same time? It made her feel hugged to think God wanted to talk to her every day.

Good morning, God.

Soon she heard the thunder of everyone's Bibles thumping shut. She held her empty hands together and bowed her head as the pastor closed in prayer.

"Good-bye, Lucy!" Rachel came over after tucking her Bible into her purse.

"See you," Lucy said. "Your song was great."

"Thanks," Rachel said, and then she was off with another girl.

When they got home, Lucy first ran to check the voice mail. *Nada,* as Serena would say.

Lucy changed her clothes and sat down at the piano for a while. After playing "California Girls" three times, she decided waiting was ridiculous.

Why shouldn't she call her best friend, after all?

She took the portable phone with her and climbed the stairs. Normally she ran. This time, she took her time.

After quietly closing her door, she sat down on her bed and dialed. One ring. Two.

"Bueno?"

Mama mia. Spanish.

"Hello, may I please speak with Serena?"

The woman let loose a flood of Spanish, none of which Lucy could understand.

"Gracias," Lucy said, recalling one of the few Spanish words she knew. No way to leave a message.

Lucy opened her Jelly Belly case and popped out two Crushed Pineapple beans and chomped on them with a Jalapeño bean. Pineapple salsa usually did the trick. This time, nothing.

Something had to give.

☂ ☂ ☂

Later that night Lucy sat cross-legged on her bed, reading Amelia Earhart's biography. Even though she'd read it once a couple of weeks ago, she'd dragged it out from under her bed again.

Someone knocked at her door.

"Yes?" She snapped the book shut and stood up. Maybe the phone had rung and she hadn't heard it!

Her mom opened the door. "Can I come in?"

Lucy quickly glanced at her mom and saw she had no phone in her hands.

"Sure." Lucy sank onto her bed again.

"I forgot to ask you, how did reading the diary go yesterday?"

"Oh that." Lucy reached out and gripped the little Woodstock tightly in her hand. "Well, we read it okay, and it seemed all right. The diary girls were going on a plane ride. Planes were kind of new then. And they liked Amelia Earhart."

Lucy's mother picked the book up from her bed. "So that's why you're reading this again, eh?"

Lucy nodded. "So we have to do something daring. I . . . uh, wanted Serena to go on Supreme Scream. But it didn't work out too well." Lucy told her mother the whole tale.

"Oh, Lucy," her mom said. "You can't try to make your friends more like you."

Lucy nodded. "I know that now, Mom. I really did think it was a good idea at the time. So then I said to her, 'Hey! You should be in the Island Art Fair. You're really good.' She seemed kind of mad at that, too, but I thought *that* was a good idea." Lucy watched her mom's reaction.

"Then the water got choppy and we got off the ferry. I haven't heard from her since."

After a short silence Lucy asked, "Well, don't you think it was a good idea? After all, you're an artist. You show your paintings. You encouraged Serena to keep it up!"

Lucy's mom stood up and said, "Yes, I'd certainly be proud of her for showing her work after she has been so hesitant. It's not easy, I know. I'm tired. You'd better get to bed, too. I love you."

She kissed Lucy's cheek and walked out of the room.

Lucy scooted the book to the side of the bed. Why hadn't her mom been more excited? Was she too tired?

Oh. An uneasy thought hit Lucy.

What if her mom thought Serena's art wasn't good enough to show, and she just didn't want to tell Lucy? Maybe Lucy really hadn't done something good for her friend, as she had promised. Lucy had been going to ask her mom to look at Serena's new painting, but now she wasn't sure.

Lucy'd better talk to Serena in the morning.

Dare

Monday morning . . . D Day minus four

The next morning, just after breakfast, Lucy called to her mom from the front door. "I'm going to Serena's for a little while, okay? Then I'm going to baby-sit Claudette."

"Okay, honey. Don't forget you promised to take some dog food over to Mrs. Marshall," Mom called back from the living room, where she was already hard at work, painting by the bright morning light. "It's right by the front door."

Sure enough, there was the bag of dog food. It wasn't a big bag and it had a handle. Lucy could lug it over on the way.

Lucy walked up the road, a boat horn honking three times in the nearby harbor. To Lucy it sounded like "Good-morn-ing."

"Good morning," she answered, clattering up the road in her flower-powers.

She pushed open the gate to Mrs. Marshall's house,

walked past the ceramic bunnies on her front stoop, and knocked.

"I'm glad to see you." Mrs. Marshall answered the door, her bright red hair fuzzed like a clown's. "And I'll bet your little puppy will be glad to see you, too."

Lucy ran over to where the little puppies squirmed with their mom, Misty. One puppy, the one with the Dr Pepper–colored ribbon around her neck, rolled backward.

"Oh, Venus!" Lucy giggled. She scooped her puppy into her hands. In a few weeks Venus would be old enough to come home with her for good. She petted Claudette's little puppy, too, in case Claudette didn't get over there today.

"I saw your friend Serena at church yesterday," Mrs. Marshall said. "She's such a nice girl."

"Yes, she is. I'm on my way over there right now."

"Well, get on with you now." Mrs. Marshall waved at her. "These pups need to go back to sleep. Thanks for the dog chow. Misty will enjoy it, and soon enough these little wiggle worms will, too."

Lucy stroked Venus's velvet fur one last time, then set her down next to her mother.

Lucy headed out the door and down a few blocks. Soon she stepped onto Marine Way. One, two, three houses, Lucy counted. Serena's was seven houses down.

Lucy stepped up to the front door and read the sign. *Saludad, Amigos.*

She reached out and knocked. Within seconds Serena opened the door. She opened her arms and hugged Lucy.

Lucy smiled and hugged her back. Another boat

honked three times in the distance. "Life-is-good!" it seemed to say.

"Come on in!" Serena said. Just inside the door stood a wrinkled woman wearing a bright red skirt. "This is Roberto's *abuela*," she said. "His grandma, remember?"

Lucy smiled and held out her hand. The old woman squeezed it hard between her own two hands, which were loaded with silver rings. Then she said something in Spanish.

Lucy looked at Serena, who answered for her and then pulled Lucy upstairs. Roberto passed them on their way up. He looked different. He started to say something, but Serena shushed him and tugged Lucy up the remaining stairs.

Serena closed the door as soon as they went into her bedroom.

"It's a little wild around here," she said. "My mom gets freaked out when Roberto's abuela visits. She hasn't been to Catalina for a long time."

"I tried to call you last night."

Serena looked surprised.

"Someone answered in Spanish, so I couldn't leave a message."

"Grandmother strikes again," Serena said. She giggled. "I was still kind of mad at you yesterday anyway."

"I guessed."

"But I'm not now, and I have news. And a daring Diary Deed for you."

Lucy's heart raced. "What's the dare?"

"First, the news." Serena settled on her yellow checked quilt. Lucy sat next to her.

"I'm going to exhibit in the art show!"

Lucy's heart struck an extra beat. Now she could *never* tell Serena about her mom's reaction. All she said was, "Really? What changed your mind?"

"Well, yesterday morning I was looking up some stuff for my Sunday school lesson—"

"Cramming at the last minute?" Lucy teased.

"Yes," Serena giggled. "Anyway, I came across this." She opened her worn Bible and started to read it to Lucy. " 'That is why I remind you to use the gift God gave you. . . . Now let it grow, as a small flame grows into a fire. God did not give us a spirit that makes us afraid. He gave us a spirit of power and love and self-control.' "

She closed her Bible.

"So all day yesterday," Serena continued, "I was thinking about it. And last night I thought, maybe I *do* have a gift. And this is one way to find out. If I win a ribbon— any ribbon at all—then I probably do. Hey! Even your mom said I should keep at it, and she should know, right?"

Lucy's stomach twisted. "Right."

"I'm going to sign up today, and I'm going to work really, really hard. I want to prove to myself that maybe I have some talent. And"—her voice lowered—"I want to prove to you that I'm brave."

"I'm really sorry about Saturday," Lucy said. "You don't have to prove anything to me. I wanted to help you, but I didn't do too well."

"I know. And even though the Supreme Scream thing wasn't helping, this is." Serena hopped up and slammed her closet door shut. "My painting is in there. I've been working on it for a little while, so I'm going to bring that one. I don't want you—or anyone—to see it till the end. A surprise."

Please, God, let the painting be terrific. And now I can't ask my mom to look at it anyway.

"Let's get a drink and sit outside," Serena said. Putty, her kitten, meowed and trailed them downstairs.

Roberto sat in the kitchen. When she thought Lucy wasn't looking, Serena held her finger up to her lips, as if to tell Roberto to be quiet again.

Strange. What's going on?

They grabbed a couple of soft drinks and went to sit on a blanket in Serena's backyard.

Serena picked some tiny daisies and began to weave them together.

Lucy balanced her can on the ground, then slid a piece of grass out by the root and chewed on the white part.

"Okay, what's my dare?"

"It has to do with Roberto." Serena didn't look up, but kept on weaving a long daisy chain.

"So that's why he's acting kind of weird today."

"Remember how I told you his band is going to play in the Art Fair?"

"Yeah."

"Well, he stayed home all day Saturday to practice with them. But when he showed up, their keyboard player said his dad had grounded him and now he isn't allowed to play."

"That was mean! It's punishing the rest of the band!"

"Yeah," Serena said. "Including Roberto, who has been

practicing for a month. They even made up their own song. And of course his abuela is here to listen to him."

"I'm really sorry," Lucy said. "But what does that have to do with me?"

Serena tied her long daisy chain into a wreath and set it nearby. "Well, Roberto heard me playing the tape of 'California Girls' you made for me. When he found out it was you playing, he had this great idea."

Uh-oh.

"Maybe *you* could play with the band this Friday." Serena smiled sweetly. "It would be a daring Diary Deed. Like mine."

"Ahhh . . . no," Lucy said. "I already told you about my awful experience a few years ago—that I froze on stage, couldn't remember how to play, had no music, and forgot the song even though I had memorized it. I walked off in the middle of the recital, totally humiliated. My mom told me I didn't have to play in public again, and I'm not going to. No way."

"But think of Roberto! Think of me!"

"I can't solve the world's problems," Lucy said. "And there weren't even judges at that recital like there are at the Art Fair!"

"The judges are nice. Jake's dad might be one of them. He was last year, but they keep them secret till the end."

"That is supposed to make me feel better? That Jake's dad—and all the rest of the Island—might witness my final humiliation?" Lucy shifted and accidentally knocked over her pop can; the Dr Pepper dribbled out onto the grass, staining the edge of the blanket.

"I'm sorry," she said, trying to wring it out.

"So"—Serena looked down at the grass—"you want *me* to do something hard but not do something hard yourself."

Lucy looked down at the grass, too. Just because it was the truth didn't make it any better. It made it worse. But not bad enough for her to agree.

"Is there even music written out for this song?" she finally asked. "I can't play a song without reading the music."

Serena looked up and smiled. "Let's ask Roberto!" She fixed the daisy wreath in Lucy's hair with an extra hair comb from her own hair, and then shouted toward the house. "Roberto!"

"I didn't say I'd do it!" Lucy grumbled. "And I hate hair combs."

Roberto came running out, as if he'd been waiting for the call.

He stood in front of the blanket, looking down at them. His black hair was neatly cut, his eyes bright with hope.

"Lucy wants to know if you have the song written down."

"I'm sure she can learn by ear." He turned to Lucy. "I heard you play. That tape was fantastic. You did a lot of things on your own."

"Thanks," Lucy said.

"Is the music for the song written down?" Serena pressed. She and Lucy both looked up at him.

He sank to his knees next to the blanket, resting on the

spot where the Dr Pepper had spilled. Even though it must have been wet, he didn't move.

"No," he said. "We just played and made it up as we went. It's not written out."

Something Old, Something New

Monday afternoon and evening . . .

"I can't play a song if I don't read the music," Lucy said. "I'm really sorry. Especially . . . especially to perform in public with it. I just can't."

Just then Serena's mom came out. "Let's go now. We're taking Abuela to the interior of the Island today, remember?"

She shooed them all into the house, her smile pinched where it was normally bright, her makeup already perfect at this time of day.

"Good-bye," Serena said softly. "I'll talk with you later."

Roberto nodded but said nothing out loud. His fallen face said it all.

Lucy, feeling lower than low, walked out the front door

and over the few blocks to Claudette's house. The town of Avalon was so small it was only a short distance from any one place to another. That was good, because today it meant she didn't have to think about Roberto's fallen face for very long.

"Come on in! I've been waiting for you!" Claudette pulled Lucy into her room.

Mrs. Kingsley poked her head into the room. "I'll be back in a couple of hours."

Claudette closed the door to her room and unleashed one of her famous jump ropes from its wall post. Lucy kicked her shoes off and sat on Claudette's bed.

"Check this out." Claudette stood in front of Lucy, twirling the rope.

> *"Sheep in the meadow,*
> *Cows in the corn.*
> *Jump on the month*
> *That you were born.*
> *January, February . . ."*

Lucy stared at the ceiling, hoping the rope wouldn't bring the light down. Finally Claudette stopped at August, her birthday month.

"Do you think I have talent?" Claudette pulled her socks up toward her knees; the right sock was yellow, the left sock pink.

"Yes, you have talent," Lucy said. "Why don't you wear two socks that are the same color?"

"It's my sunrise set," Claudette said. "I wish I could be in the Art Fair this week."

Lucy focused on Claudette. "How do you know about the Art Fair?"

"I can read the posters, silly," Claudette said. "They probably don't have a jump-roping contest, though."

"No," Lucy said. "And you're not twelve or older."

Claudette sank into the bed. "Everything fun is for older kids."

"Wouldn't you be scared?"

"No. I'm brave like you."

Oh yeah. I'm so brave.

"I really wish I could do it, though." Claudette twirled her rope around her hands.

"Why don't you have your own Art Fair?" Lucy suggested. "You and your friend Michelle." Michelle and Claudette twirled ropes together all the time.

Claudette stood up. "Do you think people would come?"

Hmm. "Well, I'll come," Lucy said.

Claudette hugged her. "Do you promise?"

"I promise."

"You always have the best ideas. Will you teach me to play 'Heart and Soul' on the piano? I want to be like you."

They sat at the piano, and Lucy taught Claudette how to play the song. After a few times through, Lucy noticed how Claudette looked at her. It was kind of like how Lucy felt about Rachel, she guessed.

It felt kind of good.

🎊 🎊 🎊

Later that evening Lucy sat in a red leather booth at King's Fish Market. Her mom and dad scrunched together across the table from her.

"Is this part of your new marriage counseling class?" Lucy joked. "You have to slam together in a booth before you show up tomorrow night?"

"Very funny, miss," her father said. "Let's order, I'm starving."

Lucy scanned the menu for something she'd wanted to order since she got to Catalina Island. *Aha*. It was on the menu.

She snapped her menu shut and looked over the water while her parents made their decision. The restaurant was perched on a long, wide dock. Rows of thin fishing line were strung up to discourage the sea gulls. Silver heat lamps brought a blush of warmth to the patio, open to one side during the summer.

"I'll have an appetizer of raw oysters," Lucy ordered when the waitress came. "And a bowl of clam chowder."

Her mom and dad stared at her before ordering for themselves. When the waitress had collected the menus and left, Mom asked, "Since when do you like raw oysters?"

"Oh, I don't know. I thought I might try—"

Suddenly, from the table behind her, Lucy heard the words *Art Fair*. She turned her head toward them.

"Yoo-hoo, Lucy," her father's voice drew her back. "I don't think they've invited us into the conversation at that table." He smiled at her as she turned back to their own conversation.

"Aw, Dad. Okay."

Lucy's raw oysters came, and she slurped them down. They tasted like . . . well, like the stuff in the back of your throat when you have a cold. But she didn't mention it to her parents.

She heard nothing more from the table behind her.

"Did I tell you that Serena's going to exhibit in the Art Fair after all?" Lucy said.

"Wonderful!" Lucy's dad seemed excited. "Your mother mentioned to me that Serena'd been thinking about it. What helped her to decide?"

"The Bible," Lucy said. She saw her parents glance at each other. She was not in the mood for a big lecture right now. She knew they'd say something. And they did.

"What a great place to find an answer." Dad cracked open a crispy piece of fish and dipped it into the tartar sauce.

"Do you really think the Bible is the same for us now as it was when it was written so long ago—that it can talk to me, personally? I mean, things are wa-a-ay different now." Lucy looked at her soup. At least she'd put her honest feelings out there.

"Do you think the diary girls are all that different from you, honey?" Mom asked.

"I guess not."

"Do you have the same kinds of feelings and problems and thoughts that they did?" Her mom smiled gently.

"Yeah, it's really amazing. Even though they talk a little differently."

Her dad smiled. "People are people, and they always have been. God knows us all inside and out, and He put just what we need into the Bible. For all of us, then and now." He ate a piece of bread. "There are interesting people in there, too. Like Jacob." He smiled.

Lucy kicked her dad under the table. "Oh, Dad! Quit it." She wiped her mouth with her napkin. "Ready to go?"

Her parents finished up, and then they paid the bill and left.

🍄 🍄 🍄

Later that night, after they'd gotten home and Lucy did her chores, Lucy flopped on her bed.

She'd meant to keep reading her Amelia Earhart book.

Instead, though, she closed her bedroom door and lifted her shrink-wrapped Bible into her hands. She slit the plastic and peeled the thin skin off. After looking at it for a minute, she opened the cover and looked inside. The printing seemed small.

She sniffed. The book smelled woodsy. And good.

In the back was a list of words and people. Her eyes caught the name *Jacob*.

Giggling, she looked up the passages about Jacob. She read them, and they seemed real and alive. *Maybe his friends called him Jake, too!*

She thought about Serena finding her answer in the Bible.

"Yes, Serena, you do have a gift," she whispered to the pages. "God's telling you, 'Don't be afraid.' "

Lucy turned to the front of the Bible, where she'd noticed some topics listed. *Worry. Anger. Help.*

Yes, I could use some help right now. Lucy ran her finger down the list to one of the page numbers and verses listed under *Help.* She flipped through the Bible, letting the thin pages pass one by one till she came to the page listed, then scanned Galatians for the right verse.

"*When we have the opportunity to help anyone, we should do it,*" it said.

She had gone looking for help and had been asked to help instead.

That verse was written to people long ago, but it was written to Lucy, too. She knew that now.

Roots

Tuesday morning . . . D Day minus three

Lucy opened the front door the next morning to snag the weekly paper for her mom and dad. When she did, she got a surprise.

An upside-down manila envelope rested on the front stoop, against the door.

Forgetting about the weekly paper, Lucy reached down and took the envelope. *Work for Dad, maybe.*

She walked back into the kitchen. "I think this is yours, Dad." She handed it over.

"That's strange. Maybe Brent had something for me. He knows we're going to the interior today to research so I won't be in the office." Dad turned the envelope over and started to open it. "You're still going with me, aren't you?"

Lucy nodded. They'd wanted to spend some more time together this summer. She and Dad. Lucy had hoped for more time alone with Mom, too, but her mom always seemed too busy.

"Wonderful." As her dad slid his finger under the seal, he stopped. "Lucy? This has your name on it." He held it out toward her.

Sure enough, in the upper left-hand corner someone had neatly printed in light, tiny letters: *Lucy.*

She sat down, pushed her cereal bowl aside, and slid her finger under the sticky seam. Once it was open, she could see there were several pages.

Lucy pulled the stack out. Music. Several pages of music, neatly printed out on a computer. In the upper right-hand corner it said, *"Dreamtime." Copyright Roberto Romero.*

She let the papers drop to the table. Now there was music to read.

"What is it, honey?" her mother asked.

"Roberto must have written out the music to his song," Lucy said.

"What?" her parents both asked at once.

"I'll be right back. And then I'll explain." Lucy padded into the living room and picked up the ancient wall phone. She dialed Serena.

"Are you awake?" she asked when Serena answered.

"No, I'm answering the phone in my sleep."

"Ha. Well, I found an envelope on my doorstep today. It has music in it."

"I know," Serena said. "Roberto stayed up all night playing the music and writing the notes down, then putting it into the computer. Yesterday he wasn't sure he could get it done in time, so he didn't tell you he'd try."

"Serena, does Roberto know about my freezing up at the recital?"

"No," Serena said. "I didn't think he needed to know."

Silence hung between them like a cliff diver in midair.

"Okay, I'll do it."

"What?"

"I'll do it," Lucy said. "I'll try, anyway. I'll play with the band, but I can't guarantee the results. I could freeze in the middle of the song again. He could end up looking like a fool in front of his abuela instead of impressing her."

"Lucy, it'll be fine. But what made you change your mind?" Serena asked.

"Last night I found my answer the same place you did," Lucy said, giggling a little. "In the Bible. It talks about helping someone whenever you get the chance, and, well, I guess I have a chance to help someone, don't I?"

"You do!"

"The music is hard," Lucy said. "And I only have three days to learn it."

"You'll do great!" Serena answered. "You have the music to read. Roberto will be ecstatic. I'm so proud of you."

The girls hung up then, promising to meet later that afternoon. Within moments Roberto called her right back to tell her, "Thanks!" Then Lucy walked back into the kitchen.

"I'm going to enter the Art Fair," Lucy said.

"You are?" Her mother looked surprised.

"Well, I'm going to play the keyboards for Roberto's band, and they're already signed up as a band, so it's not too late," Lucy said. "I decided to help out after reading my Bible last night."

"Wonderful," her dad said. Lucy wished he'd find a new favorite word.

"I've got to spend a lot of time practicing."

"You can do it. I'll be there on Friday, ready to watch you." Dad glanced over at Lucy's mother.

"You're coming, too, right, Mom?" Lucy asked.

Lucy's mother sat down. "I'm glad you're playing, honey, and I will do everything I can to be there. . . ." She hesitated. "I did make a commitment long before you'd decided to play, though. Barbara is coming this weekend. She arrives Friday."

Oh yeah. Mom's art agent. Work again. "Well, it's just for a little while," Lucy said.

"I will do everything I can to be there to watch you," her mom finished. "I promise."

"And now we'd better get ready," Dad said. "You're still coming with me to the interior this morning, right? I've got a picnic packed for us."

Lucy couldn't let him down. "Okay, Dad."

"And you're taking Claudette this afternoon for a few hours. You've already promised her mother," Mom reminded her.

Lucy sighed again. "Okay, Mom."

They got busy about their day. Lucy promised to get dressed and meet her dad on the porch in half an hour. She grabbed the envelope of music and brought it into the piano room. Hundreds of notes swam across pages of white water. Music she'd never played before.

An hour later Lucy and her dad unpacked the university's Jeep at a remote place in the interior of Catalina Island. Each summer her dad researched strange plants at various locations—he and Claudette's dad worked together. This year they were on Catalina Island. Most of their time was spent in the town of Avalon, but they often found strange plants to look at in the sea or inland.

"Put that little tent up. It'll keep the sun off of us," Dad said. Lucy popped up a light blue tarp held together with twiggy steel poles that looked like bird legs. The ground beneath was tough and dry.

She set out her chair and her dad's chair, with the cooler between them.

"Whatcha looking for today?" she asked.

"Dragon tree, lemonade berry." He got his camera ready.

Lemonade berry. Hmm. That reminded Lucy of Jelly Bellies. She opened her little travel case and popped out a Lemon Lime and a Blueberry, then chewed them together. *Tasty.*

The two of them hiked over to a short, scrubby tree that her father began to photograph.

Lucy sat down on a towel nearby. "What do you think of my playing in the Art Fair?" she asked.

"I think it's great if that's what you want to do."

"I don't really. But I do want to do something good for Roberto, like I'm doing something good for Serena. I want to be fair to Serena. And . . . and I want you and Mom to be proud of me."

"We are proud of you," her dad said. "I know how hard it is. And it might be doing something good for yourself, too."

"Hmmph." After a moment Lucy asked, "Did you ever really mess something up?" She popped out two more Jelly Bellies.

"I lost my first teaching job," Dad replied.

So he's listening after all.

"I didn't see things the way my boss did. So I told him. I thought we could work things out. Instead, he cancelled my contract on the spot."

Lucy gasped. "What happened?"

"I got depressed. I delivered pizza while I looked for another job."

"I guess you got one."

"I did. And even though it wasn't easy, it was okay. If I hadn't tried again, I'd still be delivering pizza instead of doing what I love."

Lucy looked at the scraggly little plant tickling her leg. It struggled to make its way up out of the ground. One thin stalk. Four pale leaves. But it stood straight up.

"You don't know how deep your roots are till the wind blows," Dad said. "That's a little plant joke."

"I get it, Dad."

Dad moved to another tree, but Lucy stayed put. She bent over and talked to the little plant. Talking to plants was supposed to be good for them, she'd heard. It hadn't done her houseplants any good, but maybe an outdoor plant was different.

"Do you have deep roots, little scraggler?" she asked. "I wonder if I do. I guess I'll know when the wind blows on Friday."

8

We Promise

Tuesday afternoon . . .

Later that day Lucy met Serena at the corner.

"I told my mom I'd stop off at the B.O. Box and get the mail," Lucy said.

"B.O. Box?"

"Body-odor Box instead of post-office Box. Haven't you noticed how badly the post office stinks?"

Serena giggled. "What are we going to do after that?"

"Take Claudette shopping for a while. I have to baby-sit. Then I have to stay at her house afterward, because my mom and dad are going to church tonight."

"Tonight?"

Lucy hadn't told Serena her parents were going to a marriage counseling class. It still seemed kind of personal. "Yeah, they have a class," she said.

Serena didn't ask any more. The two of them rounded the corner toward the main part of town. Streams of tourists filled the streets—shopping, tanning, eating, and laughing. All of these tourists would be there Friday afternoon, too, for the Art Fair. Lucy felt like holding on to Serena's hand in order to stay together.

They reached the post office, and Lucy opened their box and stuck the mail into her beach bag. Then the two of them headed to pick up Claudette.

"I've been painting," Serena said. "Have you been practicing?"

Lucy gulped some air. "I'll do more tonight at Claudette's. It's a cool song. And hard. Your brother is really talented."

"I hope I am, too," Serena said. "My dad is coming home early this week so he can look at my exhibit and listen to Roberto."

They knocked on Claudette's door, and Mrs. Kingsley answered. "It's not too much trouble to take her with you, is it?" she asked.

Lucy was about to say, "Yes, it is," jokingly, when she spied Claudette's little face looking around the corner.

"Nah, it's no trouble," Lucy said. "Come on, kiddo. We'll take you shopping and get you a treat before we come back." She set her bag down in the Kingsleys' entryway; inside rested the sheet music and the mail.

Claudette scurried along, her blue shirt tucked into her green shorts. Her left leg had a green sock. Her right one sported blue.

"I'm ready!"

The three of them took off downtown. First, they went into the postcard shop and bought some postcards. Lucy bought one with a talking shark for her piano teacher and a beach scene card for Katie, her cousin.

Lucy still felt a pang of guilt sometimes about not going back home to spend the summer with Katie. Besides, if she'd been home this week, she wouldn't have to play the piano in front of thousands of people.

"Find what you need?" Serena asked.

Lucy nodded and smiled. If she'd been home this week, she'd never have become such good friends with Serena . . . never have had any diary adventures . . . never have had the chance to find out how strong her roots were.

They left the shop and went down a few doors. "Can we stop in here?" Serena asked.

The three girls walked into a beach clothing shop. Whenever Lucy tried on a ring, Claudette tried on the same one. If Lucy admired a shirt, Claudette admired it right afterward. Lucy rolled her eyes.

"Ooh, I love these!" Serena found four purple hair combs. "You look good in purple, too," she told Lucy. "Here, try these on."

"I don't like hair combs," Lucy said. "I like headbands, ponytails, barrettes. But combs always slide down on me."

"They'll look great on you. Your hair looks pretty off of your face." Serena picked up two combs and slid them into Lucy's hair. Then she picked up two more and slid them into her own hair.

"Perfect! Let's get them. I'd really like us to wear them together on Friday. We'll be twins. Okay?"

Lucy nodded, then noticed Claudette watching them. Claudette went over to the hair accessories bin.

"No more combs left," Claudette said to herself.

"Come on, let's go get something at Sweet Dreams." Serena quickly paid for the hair combs before they walked out the door.

Lucy felt the teeth from the combs bite into her skull. It pinched. Soon enough they'd be sliding out of her hair. She wanted Serena to know she'd try something that Serena had picked out, too, instead of always doing her own thing. So she left them in.

As they walked down the street toward Sweet Dreams, Lucy noticed Claudette patting her hair. Then Claudette twirled a piece of her hair around her finger and blew hard on it. She did it again, and again.

"Claudette, what are you doing?"

"I want my hair to look pretty, too," she said. "I'm curling it with the heat from my breath."

Lucy turned her head quickly so Claudette wouldn't see her smile.

When they got to Sweet Dreams, they found a whole group of their friends already sitting outside eating ice cream.

They went into the pretty pink-and-yellow shop to order. Jake's mom was behind the counter; Jake sat outside with the others. Claudette and Serena ordered ice cream, and Lucy ordered a Dr Pepper.

Then they joined the kids outside, who were talking about how crowded Avalon was.

"There'll be more tourists here on Friday," someone said. "It's always so crowded on the weekend."

"And even more because of the Art Fair. I saw you signed up," Jake said to Serena.

"She's a great artist," Lucy said. "I'm glad she did."

"Lucy's going to be performing, too," Serena said.

"You are? I was just looking at the exhibitor list, and I didn't see your name."

"She's playing in my brother's band. One of the players got grounded," Serena said.

"Wow. We'll all be there to watch," Jake said. "We promise."

Lucy sucked down her Dr Pepper. "I guess I'd better take Claudette home," she said.

And practice.

☂ ☂ ☂

For supper Mrs. Kingsley made tomato soup with cubes of cheese in the bottom, served with crackers shiny with salt. Lucy loved the chubby cheese chunks, sunk like treasure on the sea floor. She'd have to tell her mom about this recipe. Or her dad.

After dinner she asked her big question. "Could I please practice at your piano?"

"Certainly," Mrs. Kingsley said.

"Can I watch?" Claudette jumped in.

"I'd rather be alone," Lucy said softly. Claudette's face dropped.

"Come on, you and I will watch a movie in the bedroom." Mrs. Kingsley aimed Claudette down the hallway while Lucy gathered her music.

She took out the envelope with the music in it. On the cover was a pencil sketch of Lucy at the piano and the words *You can do it*. It was her mom's handwriting. Lucy slipped the pages from the envelope and sat down at the piano. She was nervous about playing the piano in anyone else's house.

Maybe the Kingsleys could hear her, even down the hall.

Lucy slid the music in front of her.

She remembered Jake saying they'd all be there. *"We promise,"* he'd said.

Lucy had better get used to having other people hear her.

She put her fingers to the keys and played and played, her mind trying to connect the notes on the page with the action she must take next. It was a map to help her play something wonderful and do something good. And test her roots.

After an hour Lucy grew tired and came to a tough spot. Time after time she stumbled, not able to help her brain translate the notes on the page to the keys she must strike in the right order at the right time.

Tears filled her eyes.

Then she heard a noise. Out of the corner of her eye, she spied Claudette.

"Claudette!"

"I was just going to get some popcorn," Claudette tried to explain. "I'm really sorry about *all* those mistakes." Then she skipped away into the kitchen.

Oh Brother!

Wednesday morning . . . D Day minus two

The next morning Lucy was at the piano at dawn. "I hope the neighbors can't hear me," she muttered as she pulled the hard bench out. She'd already warned her parents of her early-morning plans.

"Good morning, God. Please let me play well now so that I can do good for someone else."

After a minute more of prayer, she played "Dreamtime" over and over.

At eight o'clock her mother brought in a glass of orange juice and a piece of toast with a pat of butter. "You need to eat something," she said. Mom smiled as she set the plate down on top of the piano. "You might as well take advantage of the fact that I'm actually serving you."

"Thanks, Mom." Lucy didn't look up from her music, didn't take her fingers off the keys. She mastered one page of notes and then stopped.

"My wrists hurt." No one was in the room to hear her;

by this time, her dad had gone to work and her mom was in the next room painting.

The lukewarm orange juice felt good trickling down her throat. She took one bite of the toast and skipped it. *Cold cardboard with an unspread lump of butter. Gross.* She should have eaten it when Mom first brought it in.

There was no time for anything else now. Her first rehearsal with the band was at noon.

Lucy put her fingers to the keys again, but her mind wandered back to the band. Would there be any other girls? Lucy wondered if Roberto had told the others that she was way younger than he was, that she was his little sister's friend. She wondered if they were all mad because their buddy James couldn't play with them, and whether they'd be angry if she didn't do it just right on Friday.

Suddenly cold crept over her, and she lost her place in the music. She put her hands on her lap and held them there, still.

Maybe what she'd meant for good would end up being really, really bad. For Serena, when she didn't win a ribbon. For Roberto, when she couldn't get through this music. For herself, when—

"Lucy? Telephone."

She rubbed her aching arms again and grabbed the phone.

Roberto spoke on the other end.

"I know, I'll be there," Lucy answered. "I'm practicing now."

She went and lay on the couch in the living room for a minute, breathing in the soothing smell of her mom's paint.

Lucy spread her arms out, and the sunlight from the front window bathed them with warmth. It felt like a sunlight massage.

Her mom, slaving to finish her work before Barbara got here, didn't even stop much to talk. Lucy sighed and went back to the piano till it was time to meet the band.

※ ※ ※

Roberto came by in his family's golf cart to pick Lucy up. They were going to the community center by the waterfront to practice on the equipment they would have to use for the Art Fair on Friday.

She clipped her two-way radio to her shorts on the way out the door. Her mother had made her promise to stay with Roberto till Lucy's dad showed up to get her at the end of the practice session. Mom had appointments all afternoon and wouldn't be home till past dinner.

Roberto chattered about anything and everything on the drive, obviously excited for the performance. When they walked into the community center, there were lots of official-looking people walking around. Stacks of paintings leaned against the wall, and in one room there were tables full of pottery.

"Serena's bringing her painting down tomorrow morning," Roberto said. Lucy looked at him and smiled. He was making small talk so she'd feel better.

When they stepped into the practice room, one other person was already there. He sat at the drums and waved his drumsticks at Roberto.

"Hey, Jeffrey," Roberto said. "Meet Lucy. She's going to be on the keyboards."

The drummer waved a drumstick in her direction this time. "Hey."

"Hi," Lucy answered. Something bugged her about the drummer. He made her nervous somehow, even though she had never met him before. He looked familiar to her.

Lucy clicked on her walkie-talkie and told her mom she'd arrived. She felt better when her mom answered.

A second later their bass player came in. Lucy waved at him, too. Then Roberto showed her back to the keyboard.

"Here it is! It's all yours."

They played the song through the first time, and Lucy made only a few small mistakes on the second page of the music. She thought that was pretty good. When she glanced out of the corner of her eye toward Roberto, though, she saw his jaw tighten. Lucy's dad's jaw did that sometimes.

Lucy's heart raced. Maybe Roberto was thinking of his abuela.

"Let's go through it again, okay?" They got through once more, and this time, Lucy played it perfectly.

Even Jeffrey clapped. "Well, shave my mustache if you didn't do it exactly right!"

"You don't have a mustache," Roberto said.

"Yeah, well, my grandpa always says that. Lucy will do fine. I can't wait for my mom and my sisters to hear us play."

"I think we have time to do it once more," Roberto

said. "Then we need to turn the practice room over to the next band."

The next band. Other bands would be performing for the ribbons and prizes, too.

The third time through, Lucy made more mistakes than she had the first time.

"I think you're tired," Roberto said. "Maybe you need to rest awhile."

"She did a good job for someone who's had the music less than two days," the bass player offered. Lucy smiled at him but didn't smile inside. She'd made at least five mistakes.

"I think your dad is here, anyway," Roberto said, pointing toward the door. He was. Dad was talking to a woman.

Lucy stared at the woman. Who was she? A realization slowly crossed her mind. She knew who that woman was. It was Julie's mom. Julie practically hated Lucy and had gone out of her way to make life miserable for her.

Lucy turned back toward the drummer, Jeffrey. All at once, she knew who he was, too.

Julie's brother.

10

Points

Wednesday afternoon and evening . . .

Lucy's heart skipped a beat as the realization settled in. Was Julie outside the hallway listening, too? Would Jeffrey hate Lucy once he found out his sister did? Had Julie even mentioned Lucy to him at all?

"Well, we won't get to practice together again," Roberto said as they cleared out. "They've got other things going on in the building till Friday. We'll just have to practice on our own."

Lucy couldn't be sure, but it seemed like Roberto was looking right at her. She took her music off the keyboard stand and slipped it back into the envelope.

Jeffrey stood up and tucked his drumsticks into his back pocket. Just then he looked at the door and called out, "Mom! Were you here the whole time? Did you come to listen to me?"

"I got to get some heavy groceries on the way home. You might as well help out for once and carry them." She herded him out the door, his head hanging like a wilted flower.

Lucy took soft steps toward the door. Once she got there, she peered down the hallway.

"Serena!" she said, overjoyed to see her best pal there. And no Julie in sight.

"How come I don't get that kind of welcome?" Lucy's dad teased.

Roberto winked at Lucy as he passed.

"My brother thought you could use some fun after practice," Serena said.

Lucy winked back at Roberto. "I promise I'll practice all night," she said as he left.

"You'd better," he said. He was joking again. At least, she hoped he was.

"I didn't know Serena was coming, so if you two girls want to walk around for a while, I'll meet you at home," Lucy's dad said. "In an hour or two."

The girls nodded, and Serena suggested they visit the arcade. "You haven't been there yet." Serena had her purple hair combs in.

Lucy shrugged. "Okay." It seemed really important to Serena for some reason.

A few minutes later they passed into a small courtyard of restaurants, shops, and a Laundromat. The arcade was next to the Hotel Metropole. Lucy thought it was the nicest hotel on the Island.

They stepped into a room of blinking lights and screaming sirens, pinballs boinging against the iron guts of the machines. A little girl ran past them, her fist clutching a trail of tickets.

"Can you win stuff here?" Lucy asked.

"Yeah, look." Serena took Lucy over to the bright glass case that held all kinds of prizes, with cards noting the ticket points required to earn them. A cute Peter Rabbit leaned against a slightly dusty Tigger, their eyes bright with hope under the case display lights. Race cars waited quietly in their boxes. Maybe someone would choose them today! There was a lot of cool hair stuff. Lucy spotted a beautiful bright purple headband. One hundred points.

Maybe if Lucy won that gorgeous thing, she could get rid of the purple hair combs, and she and Serena would still be twins.

"Wanna play Skee-Ball?" Lucy asked. The two of them ran over to the mini–bowling alleys and popped in a token. Six white balls tumbled down the gully.

Serena went first and rolled it into the fifty pointer. Lucy handed her the next ball. "Here, you keep it up!"

"Nah, we're supposed to do this together!"

Lucy got her first one into the gutter, but she did better after that.

"I do this every summer, remember," Serena said.

After a few games they had forty points between them. Better than that, though, Lucy noticed her wrists didn't hurt anymore. Her head felt light and so did her heart.

"Pinball, anyone?" Lucy asked.

The two girls chose a pinball machine. Serena worked the left lever and Lucy worked the right. The silver ball shot up the alley and bumped against the lights, the springs, the sockets. When it was all over they had another twenty points.

Lucy high-fived Serena. "Teamwork!"

Next they sat down in a two-seater car and had a car race. They raced around the track until Serena lost control of her car and smashed into Lucy's car.

"You knocked me off of the road!" Lucy giggled.

"I'm so sorry. What kind of friend am I?" Serena laughed. "But look! You have a new car."

The girls raced around the track till their time ran out. They collected their tickets and turned the game over to two waiting boys.

Eighty points.

On the way back to the Skee-Ball area, Lucy stopped to help a little boy who had dropped his tickets all over the floor.

"Can I help you?" she asked.

He nodded and bit his lip. "I hope I didn't lose any. I want one of those shiny cars."

"Ahh, you didn't lose any, fella. Here, stick them into your pocket." The boy shoved them into both his left and right pockets.

Lucy smiled at him and met Serena back at the Skee-Ball area.

See, Jesus? Whenever I have the opportunity, I do good—serve others. Thanks for telling me about that. And it wasn't always that hard.

After another couple of games, they had earned one hundred points.

"Let's buy something before we go home," Lucy said.

"Okay. You spend the points," Serena said. "I get to do this every summer."

Hooray! Purple headband—one hundred points.

When they arrived at the glass prize case, Lucy waited in line. The little guy with the ticket-stuffed pockets stood two people ahead of her. He tugged the tickets one by one from his pockets, tossing them on the counter.

"I'm sorry," the lady told him. "You looked at the wrong sign. The plastic cars are forty points. The metal cars are one hundred twenty-five."

"Oh. I don't have enough?"

Lucy watched as the boy's dad began to tell him how special the plastic cars were. Then she took one long, last look at the beautiful purple headband and thought about wearing those pokey combs.

Lucy sighed. "Here." She handed over her tickets and left the counter before the boy or his dad could say a word. And before she could change her mind.

Oh well. Guess I'll wear the silly combs on Friday.

Lucy and Serena walked toward Lucy's house. "My mom's going to be gone tonight," Lucy said. "My dad and I will probably have peanut butter and jelly for dinner."

"Roberto's abuela is cooking at my house again," Serena said. Her eyes twinkled. "My mom has lost ownership of her kitchen. Where's your mom?"

"Who knows?" Lucy said. "The gallery, probably. Something artsy, I'm sure. Her agent is coming to pick up some work this weekend."

"I wish my mom were an artist," Serena said.

Lucy said nothing for a minute. "Sometimes I wish I

liked art more. Maybe my mom and I would be closer. I wish we were closer. Especially now that I'm getting older, if you know what I mean."

"No, what?"

"Well, there's some stuff I want to talk with her about . . . woman things. You know."

"Oh yeah." They parted ways, Serena heading toward her own street as Lucy walked into her house. It was quiet. She headed right to the piano and played till her dad called her in for a peanut butter and jelly sandwich.

She sat at the table, swinging her feet. "I guess I'm ready. I guess I'll practice tonight and tomorrow and that's it."

"Worried?"

"A little."

Dad went to the counter and took out his Bible and looked something up. He tore off a piece of paper towel and wrote down a verse. "Here. Since you're reading your Bible now, I thought it might be helpful to look this up."

"Thanks, Dad." Three Bible verses in one week. Maybe it was too much for her brain to handle. But maybe it was just what her brain needed.

Lucy took the paper towel scrap with her to the piano again, then upstairs with her later. Exhausted and barely able to see straight, Lucy set the unread verse on her dresser next to the shriveling houseplant and crawled into bed.

Heavenly Help

Thursday . . . D Day minus one

The next day Lucy had "Dreamtime" at breakfast and "Dreamtime" midmorning. She had to know it perfectly.

Serena came to the door at about ten o'clock. "Get your bathing suit! Get your sunscreen! Want to go to the beach for a while? I just turned in my painting and I feel good! At least until the judging begins tomorrow, that is."

Lucy shook her head. "I'd better practice a little more. I wish I could come, though."

Serena sighed. "Okay. Maybe tomorrow after the performance we can swim together for a while. Snorkel, maybe."

"Maybe," Lucy said. Serena left the porch, and Lucy's eyes followed after her. The sun was bright and the air was light and laughter drifted up from downtown.

She turned around and closed the door behind her.

An hour later the doorbell rang again. "We're on our

way to town," Amy said. Erica stood next to Amy. "Want to come shopping with us?"

Lucy shook her head. "Sorry, I can't. I wish I could."

"We'll look for you tomorrow," Amy promised as they bounced down the steps together. This time Lucy had to hold back from slamming the door. Lucy didn't want them to think she was mad at them.

She stomped back to the piano, her wrists heavier than ever. She practiced for a while longer, then ate a cookie, nibbling the sprinkles off the top first, then taking tiny bites. The longer her snack took, the later she got back to the piano. Dad was working at the kitchen table this morning. While in the kitchen, Lucy noticed something written on the calendar for that afternoon. *Mama mia! Claudette's Junior Art Fair—two o'clock.* Lucy had almost forgotten. Good thing her mom had marked it down.

Back to "Dreamtime." At noon, when Lucy was spooning up tomato soup with cheese chunks, the phone rang again.

"Lucy!"

"Yeah?"

"It's Roberto. Great news! We can have the practice room for a little while this afternoon. Two o'clock. Don't be late, okay? One more quick run-through together."

Lucy looked at the calendar. This song had taken over enough of her life.

"Roberto, I'm not going. I made a commitment before I knew I was going to play, and I have to honor that commitment. I'm sorry."

"But, Lucy—you have to!"

"No, I don't. In fact, I'm not playing the song again till the performance. I'm sick of it!"

"Fine." Roberto's voice was short, and he hung up without saying good-bye.

Lucy went back to the piano and let the lid slam down. She gathered up the music and stuffed it back into the envelope. Then she walked up to her room and changed into something nice.

Might as well try those combs. She worked the two purple combs into her hair. One slid out, the other one stuck. She worked with the sliding one and got it firm. On her mirror was the cross sticker Claudette had given her.

"For when you're afraid," she'd said.

"I know that song as well as I'm going to know it," Lucy said aloud. "I'm tired, Jesus. My hands hurt. People are mad. People are confusing. I'm confused."

She saw the scrap of paper that her dad had given her last night. She opened it up and read: *1 Peter 4:11.* She meant to look it up, but when she checked her watch it was five minutes before two.

Lucy left the scrap where it was and ran out of the room. She grabbed her walkie-talkie and headed down the road, arriving shortly at Claudette's house. When she stepped up to the door, her watch said 2:00 exactly.

The band is practicing right now. Mad at me. Worried about tomorrow.

Claudette opened the door. "Lucy! I'm so happy you came!"

"You look really nice." Lucy wasn't sure she'd seen

Claudette in a dress before, except maybe in church. And Claudette's hair was curled.

"Did you curl your hair with your finger this time?" Lucy teased.

"Nah." Claudette's face turned pink. "My mom used the curling iron. And look. My socks match."

Lucy looked at Claudette's matching pink socks. It just wasn't Claudette.

"I did it for you," Claudette said. "You're always talking about my socks."

"What do *you* like best?"

"Well, I guess different socks."

"Then go get different socks on."

"Wait here." Claudette skidded down the hallway to her room and came back in a flash. "One pink, one purple. They go together, don't they?"

"Yes, Claudette. And it's your own style."

Claudette brought Lucy into the living room. Claudette's parents sat on a sofa. Two candles burned on a nearby table.

"Lucy!"

Lucy turned to see her friend Betsy sitting on a big stuffed chair, her braids trailing down her back. Betsy's mom stood behind the chair.

"Michelle's in the 'performance,'" Betsy explained. Michelle was her little sister. Lucy sat next to Betsy, glad to be close to a friend.

With the two moms, one dad, Lucy, and Betsy watching, Claudette began her introduction.

"Ladies and gentlemen," she started. "I mean, gentle-man."

Up front, Michelle giggled.

"Michelle and I want to welcome you to our Junior Art Fair. We want to dedicate this to Lucy, who had such a great idea."

Lucy's insides felt warm, and she smiled softly at Claudette.

"First, Michelle will show us her beadwork. Michelle is a bead artist with many years of practice."

Lucy hid a smile.

Michelle walked around the room, holding beaded geckos, ladybugs, and ponytail twists. Lucy noticed that Betsy had two small beaded twists at the tails of her braids.

Michelle explained how she had chosen the colors and how she had taken time to weave them. She also told them they would be for sale after the show. Lucy held back a giggle.

Next, Michelle introduced Claudette.

"Claudette will play 'Heart and Soul' on the piano. Claudette has a lot of talent."

Claudette sat down and spread her dress neatly over the piano bench. She played "Heart and Soul" not once, not twice, not three times, but four times in a row. Then she stood up and curtsied all the way down to her mismatched socks.

Everyone clapped. Afterward, Claudette's mom ushered them into the kitchen for punch and cookies. It was really nice that Claudette's mom was *always* there for Claudette. Jealousy scraped at Lucy's heart.

Lucy took Claudette aside. "That was really great, Claudette. I'm proud of you."

"Thanks." Claudette looked at Lucy's hair. "I see you have those cool combs in."

Lucy thought for a minute, then tugged them out.

"Here, you can have them." She smoothed Claudette's lopsided curls and put a comb on each side of her head.

"But won't Serena be really mad?" Claudette patted the combs. "Aren't you both supposed to wear them for good luck tomorrow?"

"I don't need good luck, Claudette. I need heavenly help."

Freeze!

Friday . . . D Day!

Late the next morning, Lucy wriggled into her purple-and-white dress. She and Serena had decided to dress up a little, to look a little older, since they were some of the youngest ones at the Art Fair. Her new dress was too fancy, which left this one.

In the distance she could hear a boat horn bleat four times. To Lucy it sounded like "To-day's-the-day."

Yes, it is. Lucy poured some leftover orange juice into the plant on her dresser before doing her hair.

She hadn't told Serena about giving the purple combs away yet. Instead, Lucy pulled her hair back and up into a ponytail twist and tied it with some of the leather strips and beads she'd bought from Michelle yesterday.

While she ate a bowl of Lucky Charms, Lucy said good-bye to her mother.

"I wish you didn't have work to do," Lucy said. "I don't know why Barbara had to come today." There would be at least an hour from when the ferry arrived till Lucy's performance started. *If the ferry's on time, that is,* Lucy thought.

"She planned this weekend a long, long time ago, honey," Mom answered. "And I made commitments all day that I have to keep. No one knew then that you were going to be in this performance. I will get her at the ferry and then be there to watch you. You just concentrate on the music. I know you'll do well."

Lucy's mother, all dressed up, too, kissed Lucy on the cheek. She clicked her high heels out the door and into the golf cart and went to meet the early ferry. Lucy and her dad would walk to town.

Not much later Dad poked his head into the piano room as Lucy stared at the music on the piano. "Ready to go, Sparky?"

"I'm ready, Dad." Lucy slipped her music back into the envelope and tucked it under her arm.

They locked the door behind them.

"Dad, is it goofy to pray while we're walking?"

"No. It's never goofy to pray. And you don't have to close your eyes, either."

"Will you pray for me right now?" Lucy's hands were shaking. She clasped them together as they walked down the bright street toward the already busy town.

Dad prayed for peace and success and thanked God for Lucy and her good heart to help Roberto and his friends. "That is what this is all about, right?" he asked.

"Yes. And I guess to see how deep my roots are," Lucy answered.

"You just remember First Peter 4:11. Especially the second part." He reminded her of the verse he'd jotted down on the scrap of paper towel. Lucy didn't have the heart to tell him she'd forgotten to look it up.

When they got to town, crowds were milling around already. One area of the boardwalk had been set aside for pottery displays. One display held vases with faces sculpted in the side, another had little pots with strawberries winding around them and berries carved in the clay. Each piece had a placard with the artist's name and age on it. There were only a few twelve- and thirteen-year-old artists. Most of them were seventeen or eighteen.

Lucy wondered if her name would be listed anywhere.

Half an hour later, Lucy and her dad headed toward the area set aside for paintings. "I think I want to talk with Serena alone," Lucy said. "Will you meet me in front of Sweet Dreams in half an hour?"

Lucy waited while a small crowd looked at Serena's painting, then left. Lucy stood next to her.

"Boo!"

Serena turned around. "Hey, you!" She gave her friend a quick hug.

Lucy looked at Serena's painting, sitting just like a professional's on a wooden easel. The painting was a bright rainbow over mountains, with the ocean in the background. But making up each color of the rainbow were tiny fruits. Yellow bananas, tiny green kiwi, baby apples, small clumps of grapes. If you stood far away, it looked like a simple rainbow. When you got up close, you could see it was little fruit.

"It's called *Taste the Rainbow*," Serena said. "Do you like it?"

Lucy had worried about this moment. What if she didn't like the painting at all? What would she tell Serena?

Thankfully, that wasn't a problem. "I love it. I'm so glad you decided to exhibit. This is really great."

Serena lowered her head, but her eyes sparkled. "Thanks." She pointed to her card. "I'm number 21. That means all the judges just write down scores on their cards for each painting." She grew quiet. "I'm kind of toward the end of the list. I'm afraid they'll write down better scores for everyone besides me."

"You have nothing to worry about. I bet you win best painting." Lucy regretted the words as soon as they flew out of her mouth. She didn't want Serena to be crushed.

"Hey! Where are your combs?" Serena asked. "They'd go great with that dress. Better than they do with my skirt and shirt."

"Well . . . um . . . Serena, I don't like combs. I should have just spoken up and said so, but I didn't want to hurt your feelings. They're not me. I'm sorry. I gave them to Claudette because she loves them."

Serena was quiet. "We're not twins, then."

Lucy said nothing.

"I . . . I guess I was trying to make you more like me," Serena finally said. "I'm sorry."

"Hey, I know what that's like, right? Like when I tried to force you on Supreme Scream?" Lucy said.

"It *is* kind of like that." Serena giggled. "But I'm glad we can just be ourselves."

"Yes. And we can always tell each other what we think. Sometimes it takes being friends for a while before you can do that."

Serena nodded and smiled.

Lucy said. "I'm so glad we're that kind of friends."

Another group of people came to look at Serena's painting. "I never know if they're just looking or judging," Serena said. "I'm supposed to stay by my work for another half hour. Then I'll come and watch you and Roberto."

Lucy looked at her watch. Serena was right. Half an hour. Her stomach sank, and she clutched her woven bag with the music in it.

"Okay. I'll be watching for you."

Lucy walked over and took a seat in front of Sweet Dreams, hoping her dad would show up soon.

Instead, a teenaged girl from the Christian camp came by handing out mini–New Testaments. They must have been taking the opportunity to reach the huge crowds today.

The girl stepped up to Lucy and held one of the small Bibles out to her.

"No thanks, I already have a Bible," Lucy said.

"Pass it on to someone else, then," the girl said before walking off.

Lucy set it in the bag near her music envelope with the sketch her mom had drawn. *Don't worry*. She had read the music; she could play the song. That's what she'd always told herself, right?

All at once Lucy understood. She reached into her bag again and took out the little Bible from its spot right next to her music. *Music. Bible. Music—Bible!* It was the same. Very much the same.

I can't play God's song if I don't read the music! And I have His music to read.

Lucy opened the Bible and turned to the place in 1 Peter that her dad had mentioned on the way to the Art Fair, the one he'd jotted on the piece of paper towel.

"The person who serves should serve with the strength that God gives."

She turned to the passage that she'd discovered the other night—the one that she felt like God had chosen just for her.

"When we have the opportunity to help anyone, we should do it."

Without closing her eyes or moving her lips so she wouldn't look weird, Lucy thanked the Lord for the Bible, for loving her so much that He wanted to talk with her, help her, be with her. And tell her all that in that wonderful book.

Lucy giggled when she realized she had just used her dad's favorite word in a prayer. *Wonderful!*

Help me to do a good job. Give me the strength I need.

A minute later Lucy's dad came up next to her. "Ready to go? It's nearly time."

"Yeah. I guess."

Lucy walked over to the stage as Roberto and Jeffrey were tuning up. She handed her bag to her dad and stepped up onto the platform. They were playing right after the Pixie Sticks played. Lucy's name was with the others on the card in front of the stand. *Yahoo!*

"I was getting worried about you," Roberto said. He didn't seem huffy anymore. Lucy looked to the left of the stand and saw his whole family. Mr. Romero was standing behind Roberto's abuela, who was sitting on a red folding chair. Serena stood next to her, and Serena's mom was just behind her.

Serena waved and put her hands together as if to say, "I am praying for you!"

Lucy waved back and looked over the crowd again. Julie was there, apparently as surprised to see Lucy on stage as Lucy had been to see Julie's brother at rehearsal. As soon as she caught Lucy's eye, Julie leaned over and whispered something into her friend Jenny's ear. It didn't look like it was something nice being said. Julie laughed, but Jenny looked away.

Lucy's hands started to shake again.

Somewhere out there were the judges. To the right of the stage, Lucy saw Jake and his family watching. Jake winked. Lucy blushed and waved back.

When they'd gotten everything together and tuned their instruments one last time, Roberto introduced the band. He pointed out James in the crowd as a band member.

James stood nearby looking very sad. Lucy bet both she *and* James wished he were up on stage instead of Lucy.

Lucy was trying to keep her eyes on her music stand, but she scanned the crowd one last time for her mother. Nowhere.

Mom must be buried in the crowd. Remember why you're doing this, Lucy.

Roberto gave the cue, and they began to play. A minute or so into it, Lucy relaxed and felt as if the notes were flowing from the music to her brain to her heart and then to her hands.

Lucy took her eyes off of the page for a moment, to look up and see if her mom was there.

All of a sudden Lucy couldn't remember the next notes. *Eyes on the music!* But *where* on the music? Where was her place?

Lucy played a wrong note, then two. It was so obvious. Suddenly her fingers wouldn't move at all.

The Judges

Friday afternoon . . .

On her own, Lucy would have frozen for good right then and there. She'd done it before. Now she had help.

Help, Lord! Please give me the strength I need.

Lucy scanned the music with her eyes, recognized the measure that the rest of the band was playing, and found her place in the music. Within a few beats she was back on track. Her hands felt at home on the keyboard again.

Roberto was singing, of course, so she couldn't hear him breathe a sigh of relief. She knew he was thinking it, though.

Strangely, Lucy felt better after having made her mistake. She recovered. She froze—and then found her place again. She didn't have to be perfect.

The rest of the song flowed, and Lucy enjoyed the music, too. When the crowd started to clap along with the beat, she was really jazzed.

"One more time through the chorus," Roberto said,

something they hadn't planned. The band got into it, though—even Lucy.

And when the song was over, the applause went on for a long, long time. Lucy looked at her dad, who gave her a thumbs-up. Serena waved wildly. Julie even clapped politely. And Jake, at the sideline, put his fingers into his mouth and whistled.

They cleared their gear off the stage so the next band could set up. Lucy turned off the keyboard, slid her music next to the little Bible in her bag, and walked offstage. She tried to squeeze through the crowd to get near her dad. As she did, she heard Jake's dad talk to him.

"You can hang out with the others, but meet me back here when the winners are announced, okay, Chief?"

Chief! Lucy turned away and held back a giggle.

She finally reached her dad. He gave her a big hug. "You did great, Sparky."

"I made a mistake, Dad." Then the two of them sat on a small bench next to the water. The breeze blew over her sweaty skin, cooling her down. For some reason the boat horns were quiet now.

"I didn't even hear your mistake," Dad said. "Honest. I'll bet no one heard it."

Lucy held her breath, then asked, "Was Mom here?"

"I know she's here somewhere, and I'll bet anything that she heard you. But she wasn't standing by me."

"Maybe she didn't hear." Lucy's heart sank. "Is it okay if I go hang out with Serena and the other kids?"

"Yes. I'll look for the Kingsleys," Dad replied. He spied Serena. "There's Serena. You two stay together, and I'll meet you back here for the awards ceremony in an hour, okay?"

Lucy nodded.

Serena came running toward her, arms open. "You did it! And you were fabulous."

Lucy smiled. At least she hadn't said "wonderful."

"Oh, Roberto's abuela was so excited, too. Roberto really hopes that you guys will win an award. He wants to win Best Group."

Lucy thought about her frozen moments. "Oh."

Serena said nothing about Lucy's mistakes, and Lucy didn't mention them, either. Maybe Serena hadn't noticed. Maybe no one, including the judges, had noticed.

"Look! Everyone's over by Sweet Dreams. Want to go over?"

"Yes," Lucy said, making sure her ponytail twist was tight. She looked down at her dress. Purple *was* one of her best colors.

"Do I look okay?" Serena asked. Lucy remembered that one of the boys in the crowd was Serena's scuba-diving friend who had taken their picture for Lucy's birthday.

"You look great," Lucy said, not even teasing her friend a little.

They sat down at two of the open chairs at their friends' table.

"Hi, Dr Pepper," Jake said, using his nickname for Lucy.

"Hi, Chief," Lucy teased back. Jake's eyes flew open as she said that.

"Hey! Where did you hear that?"

Everyone razzed him about being the Chief of the Ice-Cream Patrol.

All of them congratulated Lucy and Serena, hoping along with them that they'd each earn awards.

As they sat chatting and drinking down malts and sodas, Jake leaned over toward Lucy and said in a soft voice, "I heard your mistakes."

Lucy's face turned red, but she didn't turn away. So they weren't so secret after all. And if Jake had heard her mistakes, his dad had, too.

"I only wanted to mention it," Jake continued, "because I heard how you kept going. I really respect that more than if you'd never even messed up. I wanted you to know that."

Lucy's grip on her Dr Pepper can relaxed. "I'm learning that," she said. "And I had a lot of fun."

Jake smiled.

The group of them decided to walk around together and see the rest of the exhibits before the awards were announced. First they looked at all of the paintings.

"Look, there are some people looking at yours," Lucy said. "And not all the other ones."

"Well, *everyone* heard you," Serena said. "It was great."

"Not everyone," Lucy said. "Not my mom."

Serena looked up. "Are you sure? I'm sure I saw your mom during your performance. Let's see if we can find her as we're walking around. It might be hard. The crowd has gotten even bigger."

The whole crew of them looked over the watercolors and oil paintings and pictures made of little scraps of paper all glued together. They went through the pottery area again, and also through the jewelry tent. Lucy looked over the rings, wishing she could make jewelry.

"Hey, we'd better get back," Jake said. "I think it's time to announce the winners."

They strolled back toward the stage where Lucy and all the others had performed. The instruments had been cleared away; now there was just a podium and a table full of ribbons.

Lucy looked around. Roberto was close to the stage. Lucy hoped he wouldn't be disappointed after everything. His abuela stood right next to him.

Lucy's dad came alongside her and chatted with Serena's father, who also stood nearby.

Soon the woman in charge came on stage.

"I'd like to thank all of this year's participants," she said. "It's our largest turnout ever, and the breadth of talent is simply amazing. So thank you, artists."

The woman cleared her throat. The harbor was behind her, the water glistening, the boats still sliding through the water.

Lucy scanned the crowd again, looking for one face in particular.

"And now I'd like to introduce our judges. We asked some of the finest people in our community this year to help us, and they have made quite a commitment. Besides bringing their considerable talent and experience, many had to spend time this week looking over the entries, going over the rules with other judges, and helping in other ways. To our many judges, please come up here and take a bow!"

Lucy looked to her left, wishing the formalities would get over. Serena elbowed her hard.

"Lucy!"

Lucy's eyes were drawn back to the stage, and her mouth dropped open.

Her mother was on stage with the judges!

"What is going on?"

Two F Notes

Friday afternoon . . .

"Dad, Mom is on stage with the judges!"

Lucy's dad nodded and smiled, then turned his head toward the stage. The speaker continued talking.

She introduced several judges, then got to Lucy's mother.

"We're so pleased to have noted artist Victoria Larson with us this year. You may not have met her, but you've certainly seen some of her work in various magazines and on book covers. Several of her pieces will be shown at our own gallery throughout the summer, as she is staying this summer on Catalina Island." The speaker then pointed to Lucy's mother's agent.

"And with her is my good friend Barbara Kitneck. Barbara and I have been friends for many years through our work at the Los Angeles Art Institute. It is through her connections there that many of today's prizes have been donated. And without her, we may not have known about Victoria Larson."

The crowd clapped but Lucy was still in a daze. Her mom was an art judge.

Had her mom judged Serena's work? Did she give it good marks? She wouldn't help Serena win a prize just because she was Lucy's friend, would she?

They introduced the music judges, pottery judges, and handcraft judges. The judges sat in two small, tidy rows to the side of the stage. Jake's dad was *not* one of the music judges! Had the other judges heard Lucy's mistake? Would they count it against the band?

Now it was time to announce the awards.

"First, the hand art."

Lucy sighed. *Yeah, yeah, get on with it. Jewelry, okay. Come on.*

"Next," the speaker announced, "we will look at the lovely pottery examples."

Lucy was pleased when one of the pretty strawberry pots won the top award. But the pottery part was still taking too long.

"Next, the music awards."

Lucy pulled close to her dad. Roberto stood with his hand on his abuela's arm.

"All of our participants were wonderful, but we can offer only three awards. Best Group will win five hundred dollars. Best New Song wins the song a preview with a music executive. And Best Overall will play at the end-of-summer party. Ready for the awards?

"First, Best Group. The Pixie Sticks!"

Of course, the all-girl band. Lucy sneaked a look at Roberto. His face hadn't changed, but he looked kind of stiff.

The Pixie Sticks went forward to claim their prize. Everyone clapped, even Lucy. They *were* really good.

"Next, Best New Song. 'Dreamtime,' written by Roberto Romero."

"Hey, he won!" Lucy's dad said.

"He won!" Lucy echoed. "He won a prize!" Roberto was already halfway to the stage. His abuela was clapping so hard her silver rings clacked together. Even Julie whistled as the band headed toward the stage.

Lucy got up on stage with the others, and as she did, she noticed her mom with a huge smile that never faded. Lucy's mom was the last judge to stop clapping and sit down.

Roberto was pulled aside and given information about sending his song to a music executive. It was possible that someone would buy the song and a famous group could record it!

Another band won Best Overall, but Lucy didn't care.

Serena hugged her after they'd returned from the stage. "It's all because of you, you know," she said. "He couldn't have won it without you."

To Lucy's shock, Roberto hugged her, too. "If you hadn't made me write down the music," he whispered, "I'd have nothing to send them. Thanks!"

Lucy hadn't ever seen a teenaged boy cry before. She couldn't be sure this time, either, but it seemed like Roberto had a tear in his eye.

Now it was time to announce the painting awards.

"My stomach hurts," Serena said. Lucy reached over and squeezed her friend's hand.

"In spite of the many lovely works of art we have, and our great appreciation to the participants, we have only two awards at this time. Best Picture and Most Promise. I'd like to introduce our winner of the Best Picture award, who wins five hundred dollars. This artist's work, *Watercolor Windows*, shows unique talent, and we are very pleased to have sixteen-year-old Richard Smarks as an Avalon resident."

Oh no. Lucy clapped, but her hands felt heavy again, like when she'd been practicing too much. *Taste the Rainbow* hadn't won.

Serena held her head low. She turned, as if she was ready to walk away from the stage. The ceremony was nearly over.

"This year, our award for Most Promise goes to someone young. The award is a gift certificate for lessons at the Los Angeles Art Institute this fall, when classes resume. We're pleased to give this award to a member of a longtime Catalina family. Serena Romero, for *Taste the Rainbow*!"

A smile grew on Serena's face, and Serena went forward. Lucy kept her eyes on her mother and Barbara. Barbara was really into the Art Institute. She had probably arranged for this prize.

Lucy's stomach felt a little queasy now.

Serena accepted her award, then stepped down from the stage. As the speaker concluded the ceremony, Serena whispered to Lucy, "I would have rather won this one than the other one anyway. I *do* have a gift. And this prize will help me to 'fan it into flames,' like the Bible said."

"You deserve it," Lucy said. "I want to go and talk with my mom, all right?"

"Meet me at the beach in half an hour, okay?" Serena said. She opened up her bag. "I brought the old diary, since I promised you yesterday morning that we'd go to the beach after the Art Fair. We have to see if the diary girls did okay on the airplane or not, right?"

"Right," Lucy agreed. "And I brought *our* diary. I'll meet you later."

Then Lucy and her dad headed over to the stage, where her mom was just finishing a conversation.

"Let's go and get a Dr Pepper," her mom said. "You did wonderfully!"

"Did you see me, Mom? Did you watch me?"

"Yes, I did. I stood in the back," Mom said as they headed toward Sweet Dreams. "I told them that I must stop all official duties at that time and only watch you."

Lucy said nothing, knowing the smile on her face said it all.

"I'll get something for us to drink," Dad offered, pointing at the long line coming from Sweet Dreams. "You ladies hold down the table till I get back."

Lucy and her mother sat at a heart-shaped iron table outside the store. Three people had just gotten up, leaving three padded seats just for them.

"Why didn't you tell me you were going to be a judge?" Lucy asked.

"I wasn't allowed to," her mother said. "Barbara has been involved in this for a long time. It was one of the reasons she wanted to come this weekend. She's very involved in helping young artists."

Young artists like Serena, Lucy thought.

"So," Mom continued, "she asked me if I'd like to help, knowing it would be good publicity for my work on the Island. And I said yes. It's neat that we could both serve when someone needed help." Her eyes sparkled.

Lucy giggled. She wondered why she hadn't noticed before today just how pretty her mom really was.

"But they wanted me to keep it quiet till the end. They don't want anyone trying to influence the judges, because it might make for unfair decisions."

Unfair decisions. Hmm.

"But I was always sure I would find a way to watch you." She patted Lucy's hand. "And I really liked your song."

"But you don't like rock music!" Lucy said.

"No, but I like you," her mom said. They laughed together. "I know that we both want our relationship to be a little different. I . . . I've been working a lot. But we will plan more ways to be together. I have one very special way planned for next week."

"What is it?" Lucy said.

"A mystery," her mother said. "A trip. An adventure. Your past. Something you'll never guess. And it might even include Serena."

A mysterious adventure with her mom and Serena. Wow!

"Speaking of Serena," Lucy said, checking her watch, "I'm meeting her at the beach in about twenty minutes."

"Good," Mom said. "I loved her painting. So did others, apparently. I didn't vote on her painting because I know her. The other scores were averaged. But I was proud when the others voted for her."

"So she won fairly, then, right? Without any unfair help?"

"She won fairly," her mother agreed. "I didn't vote, and even Barbara doesn't know that I know her."

Joy flooded Lucy's heart. Of course her mom would do the right thing! When Dad came back, she chugged down her Dr Pepper in two swigs.

"Gotta run. Serena's waiting. I'll be home in an hour or so."

"Take your walkie-talkie," her mother said. "And be home in time for dinner. I told Barbara how much you like raw oysters, and she bought a whole dozen for the two of you to split for dinner."

Lucy tried to keep her disgust about the oysters off of her face before she headed toward the beach.

She found their favorite spot, Serena already sitting there on the sand.

"Got the diary?" Lucy kicked her flower-powers off and sat next to her friend.

"Of course," Serena said. She held her certificate in her hands. "I really won. And it's all because of you."

"Nah," Lucy said.

"Yes," Serena said. "If you hadn't encouraged me, even when I was mad at first, I never would have tried."

"I guess I learned the difference between encouraging you with the right things and pushing you to be someone you're not," Lucy said. "Which is just what you did for me. *You* should take a bow!" The two of them got up and bowed toward each other, then fell back laughing.

Lucy dropped her bag onto the sand. She looked at the tiny Bible that was still inside. "It's cool that something written so long ago was written for me, too."

"Do you mean the diary or the Bible?" Serena asked.

"Both," Lucy said, digging her toes into the sand. She tapped the Bible. "Can't play the song if I don't read the music."

Serena smiled. "Let's open the diary."

Serena took one of the tiny yellow drink umbrellas out of her bag.

Lucy giggled. Serena had saved them.

Serena read first.

"Well, Diary, I was worried that things would be tricky. We stood on the side of the plane, and they lowered the stairs for us to climb up. 'We're going to die,' I whispered. 'Don't be a Dumb Dora,' Joey said. 'We'll be fine.' And we are! Here I am writing about it."

The writing changed to curly loops, and Serena handed the diary over to Lucy.

"It was fantastic, Diary. We saw like birds see—saw things that most people never see. Moun-

tain tops, whale pods swimming just under the sea. We saw things most people don't because they're afraid to try. Even Serena laughed. And she felt good, because she'd been looking for a way to serve Joey, as our Sunday school verse last week taught. She not only did so, she had fun herself."

Lucy smiled and handed the diary over to her best pal. Serena read the last words on the page.

"Ta ta! We've got secret gifts planned. We'd better go and get them ready.

Faithful Friends,
mary and Serena."

Then Serena opened up their own summer diary. After they wrote about their week, Lucy said, "I want to add one more thing."

She took the book and the pencil in hand and drew in a measure of music. Then she drew two notes. "This is our music, yours and mine," she said to Serena.

"I don't read music. What does it mean?" Serena asked.

"It's two F notes," Lucy said, pulling closer to her friend. "It's you and me. Faithful Friends!"

Serena smiled. With their work happily behind them, two Faithful Friends ran together to the edge of the water to dunk their toes in the cool surf.

The grass withers,
and the flowers fade,
but the word of our God
stands forever.

ISAIAH 40:8 (NLT)

SANDRA BYRD took years and years of piano lessons, and she did actually freeze in the middle of a recital once! Now she plays a duet at home with her daughter once in a while. Mostly, though, listening is the way she lets music speak to her "heart and soul."

Sandra lives near beautiful Seattle, between snow-capped Mount Rainier and the Space Needle, with her husband and two children (and let's not forget her Australian shepherd, Trudy). When she's not writing, she's usually reading, but she also likes to scrapbook, listen to music, and spend time with friends. Besides writing THE HIDDEN DIARY books, she's also the author of the bestselling series SECRET SISTERS.

For more information on THE HIDDEN DIARY series, visit Sandra's Web site: *www.thehiddendiary.com.* Or you can write to Sandra at

Sandra Byrd
P.O. Box 1207
Maple Valley, WA 98038

**Don't miss book five
of THE HIDDEN DIARY,
*Pass It On!***

For a preview of Lucy and Serena's next diary adventure, just hold up this page in front of a mirror.

An urgent letter arrives just as Lucy and Serena are about to leave for the mainland on a little adventure. The diary girls found a way to secretly give good things, so Lucy and Serena want to do the same. But doing good is not always as easy as it might seem.

Answering Questions
From Girls Just Like You!

GIRL TALK
by SANDRA BYRD

As you can tell from THE HIDDEN DIARY series, **Sandra Byrd** knows your likes and dislikes. She especially loves interacting with the girls who read her books. In *Girl Talk*, Sandra's created a devotional that includes answers to questions written by real girls from across the country.

- 🌸 **Why do I look different all of a sudden?**
- 🌸 **Could terrorists really blow up my school?**
- 🌸 **Do you think parents love some children more than others?**
- 🌸 **How do you know the Bible is real?**

◆ BETHANYHOUSE

Plus, True–&–False quizzes at the start of each section let you participate right along with the book!